"I thought we might get married."

Chessie had a curious feeling that the entire world had come to a sudden halt. "I'm sorry," she said at last. "I don't think I quite understand."

"It's perfectly simple. I've just proposed to you—asked you to become my wife." Miles sounded totally cool about it. "Look on it, if you want, as a new kind of contract."

Her lips moved. "Marriage is—hardly a business arrangement."

"I'd say that depends on the people involved." His gaze was steady. "Considering our individual circumstances, marriage between us seems a sensible idea." He paused. "I think we could work out a perfectly satisfactory deal."

Sara Craven

HIS CONVENIENT MARRIAGE

Wedlocked!

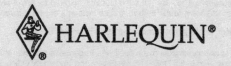

HARLEQUIN®

TORONTO • NEW YORK • LONDON
AMSTERDAM • PARIS • SYDNEY • HAMBURG
STOCKHOLM • ATHENS • TOKYO • MILAN • MADRID
PRAGUE • WARSAW • BUDAPEST • AUCKLAND

ISBN 0-373-12417-1

HIS CONVENIENT MARRIAGE

First North American Publication 2004.

CHAPTER ONE

'CHESSIE—oh, Chess, you'll never guess what they're saying in the post office.'

Francesca Lloyd frowned slightly, but her attention didn't waver from her computer screen as her younger sister burst into the room.

'Jen, I've told you a hundred times, you're not supposed to come to this part of the house, and especially not during working hours.'

'Oh, nuts.' Jenny perched on a corner of the big desk, pushing aside some of the neat piles of paper to make room for herself. 'I simply had to see you. Anyway, The Ogre won't be back from London for hours yet,' she added airily. 'I checked that his car wasn't there before I came round.'

Chessie's lips tightened. 'Please don't call him that. It's neither kind nor fair.'

'Well, nor is he.' Jenny pulled a face. 'Besides, you may not need this job for much longer.' She took an excited breath. 'I heard Mrs Cummings telling the post mistress that she's had instructions to open Wenmore Court again. And that means that Alastair's coming back at last.'

Chessie's fingers stilled momentarily on the keyboard. For a moment her heart leapt, painfully—almost brutally.

She kept her voice even. 'Well, that's good news for the village. The house has been closed up for far too long. But it won't make much difference to us.'

'Oh, Chess, don't be silly.' Jenny gave an impatient sigh. 'It makes all the difference in the world. After all, you and Alastair were practically engaged.'

'No.' Chessie turned on her. 'We were *not*. And you've got to stop saying that.'

'Well, you would have been if his beastly father hadn't sent him to business school in the States,' Jenny retorted. 'Everyone knows that. You were crazy about each other.'

'And much younger, too.' Chessie began typing again. 'And a hell of a lot has happened since then. Nothing's the same.'

'Do you really think that would make any difference to Alastair?' Jenny demanded scornfully.

'I think it might.' It still hurt to remember how the weekly letters had dwindled to one a month, and then petered out altogether before the end of their first year apart.

Since then, her only contact had been a brief note of condolence following her father's death.

And if Alastair had known that Neville Lloyd had died, then he almost certainly knew the circumstances of his death, she thought, wincing.

'God, you can be a real drag sometimes,' Jenny accused. 'I thought you'd be thrilled. I ran all the way home to tell you.'

'Jen, we shouldn't make assumptions.' Chessie tried to speak gently. 'After all, it's been three years and a lot of water under the bridge. We're not the same people any more, Alastair and I.'

There'd been a time when she'd rejoiced in those three words, she thought sadly. When they'd had meaning—even a future...

She squared her shoulders. 'And now I've got to get on. Please don't let Mr Hunter come back and catch you here again.'

'Oh, all right.' Jenny slid mutinously off the desk. 'But how great it would be if Alastair asked you to marry him. Imagine being able to tell The Ogre what to do with his rotten job.'

Chessie stifled a sigh. 'It is not a rotten job,' she returned levelly. 'It's good, and well paid. It keeps food in our mouths, and a roof over our heads. And it allows us to go on living in our old home.'

'As servants,' Jenny said with intense bitterness. 'Big deal.' And she went out, slamming the door behind her.

Chessie sat very still for a moment, her face troubled. It was disturbing that even after all this time, Jenny had not been able to come to terms with the admittedly devastating change in their circumstances.

She could not seem to cope with the fact that Silvertrees House no longer belonged to them—or that the only part of it they were entitled to occupy was the former house-keeper's flat.

'Yet, why not?' Chessie asked herself, wryly. 'After all, that's what I am—the housekeeper.'

'I don't want, or need, a lot of staff,' Miles Hunter had told her at that first, fraught interview. 'I require the house to be run efficiently, and without fuss, plus secretarial support.'

'Meaning what, precisely?' Chessie looked impassively back at her potential employer, trying to weigh him up. It wasn't easy. His clothes, casually elegant, were at odds with the harshly etched lines of his face, accentuated by the scar that ran from his cheekbone to the corner of his unsmiling mouth. The cool drawl gave nothing away, either.

'I use a very old portable typewriter, Miss Lloyd. I always have, but my publishers now require my manuscripts on computerised disks. I presume you can handle that?'

She nodded wordlessly.

'Good. On the domestic side it will be up to you what additional assistance you require. I imagine you'll need a daily help at least. But I insist on peace and quiet while I'm writing. I also value my privacy.'

He paused. 'I'm aware this may be difficult for you. After all, you've lived at Silvertrees all your life, and you're used to having the free run of the place. That, I'm afraid, can't happen any more.'

'No,' Chessie said. 'I—I can see that.'

There was another brief silence. 'Of course,' he said,

'you may not wish to take the job on, but your lawyer felt it could solve a number of problems for both of us.'

The blue eyes were vivid against the deep tan of his thin face. 'So, how about it, Miss Lloyd? Are you prepared to sacrifice your pride, and accept my offer?'

She ignored the note of faint mockery in his voice. 'I can't afford pride, Mr Hunter. Not with a young sister to support, and educate. I'd be more than grateful for the job, and the accommodation.' She paused. 'And we'll try not to impinge on your seclusion.'

'Don't just try, Miss Lloyd. Succeed.' He drew the file on the desk in front of him towards him, signalling the interview was ending. As she rose he added, 'I'll get my lawyers to draw up the necessary lease, and contract of employment.'

'Is that really necessary?' There was dismay in her voice. 'It sounds a bit daunting. Couldn't we have some kind of—gentleman's agreement?'

His mouth seemed to twist harshly, or was it just the scar that gave that impression?

'I've never been a gentleman, Miss Lloyd,' he remarked. 'And appearances are against you, too. I think it better to put things on a businesslike footing from day one—don't you?'

And that, Chessie thought drearily, had been that. She was allowed to occupy the former housekeeper's flat, with Jenny, for a peppercorn rent, as long as she continued to work for Miles Hunter.

At the time, desperate as she had been, bleak with guilt and grief over her father, it had seemed a lifeline. Too good a proposition to turn down.

Now, with hindsight, she wondered if she should have refused. Taken Jenny and herself far away from old memories—old associations.

But that would have meant finding a new school for Jenny just before an important exam year, and she'd been loth to create any more disruption in her sister's life.

And at first it had seemed worth it. Jenny had done well, and was expected to go on to university in due course. She'd get a student loan, but it would still mean all kinds of extra expenditure.

So Chessie seemed contracted to several more years of transferring Miles Hunter's starkly exciting thrillers onto the computer, and keeping his home running like the clockwork he demanded.

It had not, she reflected, been the easiest of rides. As she'd suspected at that first meeting, he wasn't the easiest person in the world to work for. He expected consistently high standards, and could be icily sarcastic and unpleasant if these were not met, as several of the daily helps who'd come and gone could vouchsafe.

But while Chessie had adhered strictly to her own territory outside working hours, Jenny had not always been so scrupulous.

She'd made it plain she regarded Silvertrees' new owner as little more than an interloper in what was still her own home, and this had led to trouble, and almost confrontation, on more than one occasion. And this had led to her coining the resentful nickname 'The Ogre' for Miles Hunter.

Chessie pushed back her chair, and wandered over to the window, beset by sudden restlessness.

Jenny could be disturbingly intolerant at times, she thought ruefully. It was true that she'd found her father's disgrace and subsequent death traumatic in the extreme, but that was no longer a valid excuse. But her young sister bitterly resented the collapse of her comfortable, cushioned life.

She wanted things back the way they were—and that was never going to happen.

I've accepted it, Chessie thought sadly. Why can't she?

And now Alastair might be returning and Jenny had seized on this as a sign that their circumstances were about to change for the better in some miraculous way.

Chessie sighed under her breath. Oh, to be that young and optimistic again.

As she had been once—when she and Alastair had been together, and the world and the future had seemed to belong to them.

As a first love, she supposed, it had been pretty near idyllic. A summer of walks, and car rides; of swimming and playing tennis, and watching Alastair play cricket. Of kisses and breathless murmurs. And promises.

In retrospect, all very sweet. And absurdly innocent.

Alastair had wanted her. There was little doubt about that, and to this day she didn't know why she'd held back. Maybe it had been some unconscious reluctance to take the step that would have left her girlhood behind for ever, and made her a woman. Or, more prosaically, perhaps it had been the fear that it had only been her body that he'd really wanted. And that, having made the ultimate commitment, she would have lost him.

'A man will tell you anything, darling, if he's trying to get you into bed.' Linnet's husky voice, cloying as warm treacle, came back to haunt her. 'Don't make it too easy for him.'

Chessie had reacted with distaste at the time. But maybe the words had stuck just the same. Like so many of Linnet's little barbs, she reflected ruefully.

And if the Court really was being re-opened, that would mean that Linnet would be back too, proving that every silver lining had a black cloud hovering.

In a way, it had been Linnet who had unwittingly drawn Chessie and Alastair together originally.

Sir Robert Markham, like Chessie's father, had been a widower for several years. It had been popularly assumed in the village that if he remarried, his choice would be Gail Travis, who ran the local kennels, and whom he'd been escorting to local functions for the past year.

But one night at a charity ball he'd seen Linnet Arthur, an actress who, up to then, had made an erratic living from modelling, bit parts in soap operas, and playing hostess on daytime television game shows. Linnet, with her mane of blonde hair, perfect teeth, endless legs and frankly voluptuous body, had been decorating the tombola. And suddenly poor Mrs Travis had been history.

After an embarrassingly short courtship, Sir Robert had married Linnet, and brought her down to the Court.

The shock waves had still been reverberating when he'd given a garden party to introduce her to the neighbourhood. And Alastair, standing like a statue in the background, had clearly been the most shocked of all.

He'd disappeared during the course of the afternoon, and Chessie had found him sitting under a tree by the river, throwing stones into the water. She'd been about to creep away, convinced he'd wanted to be alone, but his face, white with outrage and misery, had stopped her in her tracks.

Over six feet tall, with chestnut hair, and good looks to die for, Alastair, three years her senior, had always been Chessie's god.

Somehow, she'd found the courage to say, 'Alastair, I'm so sorry.'

He glanced up at her, his brown eyes glazed with pain. 'How could he?' he burst out. 'How could he have put that—bimbo in my mother's place? God, Chessie, she even brings bimbos into disrepute.'

To her horror, Chessie found herself struggling not to laugh. Alastair noticed, and his own mouth twitched into a reluctant grin. After that Linnet was always referred to between them as 'The Wicked Stepmother', and they spent many enjoyable hours slagging off the time she devoted to her personal appearance, her horrendous schemes for redecorating the Court, firmly vetoed by Sir Robert, and her doomed attempts to establish herself as the lady of the manor.

After that, they devoted themselves to devising a range

of eventual fates for her more ghoulish and grisly than even the Brothers Grimm could have imagined.

'Thank God I'm going to university,' Alastair declared eventually, with scornful resignation. 'And I won't be coming back for vacations, if I can help it.'

Chessie missed him when he went, but she was soon absorbed in her school work, planning ahead for a career in her father's company.

It was three years before they encountered each other again. Chessie, newly returned from a month living as an au pair in France, had been asked to help on the white elephant stall at the church fête, held annually in the grounds of Wenmore Court, and one of the few village events with which the new Lady Markham sulkily allowed herself to be associated.

It was a blazingly hot afternoon, and Chessie was wondering when she could legitimately sneak off and go for a swim in the river, when Alastair halted beside the stall.

'My God, Chessie.' He was laughing, but there was another note in his voice too. 'I'd hardly have known you.'

But I, she thought, the breath catching in her throat, I would have known you anywhere. *Anywhere*.

It was as if all her life until then had been geared for this one brilliant, unforgettable moment.

They stood there, smiling at each other, almost foolishly. Momentarily oblivious to everything and everyone around them. Then Alastair said quietly, 'I'll call you,' and she nodded, jerkily, afraid of showing her delight too openly.

They were practically inseparable in those first weeks of reunion, talking endlessly. She'd just left school, and was preparing to join her father in the City the following September, initially as a junior dogsbody, styled personal assistant.

Alastair, they both presumed, would do the same—start learning the family electronics business from the bottom rung of the ladder.

The weather was hot, one perfect day spilling into another, and Chessie found herself spending a lot of time at the Court, where Linnet had managed to persuade her husband to install a swimming pool.

Until then, Chessie had been too insignificant for Lady Markham to notice, but she could hardly continue to ignore her when they were occupying adjoining sun loungers.

'Hi,' she drawled, eyes hidden behind designer sunglasses, and her spectacular figure displayed in a bikini one centimetre short of indecent. 'So you're Ally's little holiday romance. How nice.'

Chessie bit her lip. 'How do you do, Lady Markham?' she returned politely, touching the languidly extended fingers.

'Oh, Linnet—please.' The red mouth curled into a smile. 'After all, sweetie, we're practically the same age.'

Back to the Brothers Grimm, Chessie muttered under her breath as she turned away.

She'd have preferred to avoid Linnet altogether during her visits, but this proved impossible. To Chessie's embarrassment the older woman had immediately recognised the fact that she was still physically innocent, and enjoyed bombarding her with a constant stream of unwanted intimate advice, like poisoned darts.

But nothing Linnet could say or do had any real power to damage her happiness. Or her unspoken hopes for the future.

That came from a totally unexpected direction.

When Sir Robert announced that he was sending his son to business school in America, it was like a bolt from the blue. At first, Alastair seemed determined to fight his father's decision, but when Sir Robert remained adamant, his mood changed to coldly furious acceptance.

'Can't you make him listen?' Chessie pleaded.

'It's no use, darling.' Alastair's face was hard. 'You don't know my father when his mind's made up like this.'

It was true that Chessie had only ever seen the genial,

open-handed side of Sir Robert. This kind of arbitrary behaviour seemed totally out of character.

'But I'll be back, Chessie.' He stared into space, his face
set. 'This isn't the end of everything. I won't allow it to
be.'

And I believed him, thought Chessie.

She hoped it wasn't some subconscious conviction that
one day he'd return to claim her that had kept her here in
the village. Because common sense told her she was crying
for the moon.

If Alastair had been seriously interested in her, if it had
been more than a boy and girl thing, then he'd have asked
her to marry him before he'd gone to the States, or at least
begged her to wait for him. She'd made herself face that a
long time ago.

It had been obvious that everyone in the neighbourhood
had been expecting some kind of announcement. And even
more apparent that, once he'd departed, people had been
feeling sorry for her. The sting of their well-meant sympathy had only deepened her heartache and sense of iso-
lation.

As had the attitude of Sir Robert, who'd made it coldly
clear that he'd regarded it as a transient relationship, and
not to be taken seriously. While Linnet's derisive smile had
made Chessie feel quite sick.

She'd never realised before how much the other woman
disliked her.

She'd wondered since whether Sir Robert, a shrewd busi-
nessman, had divined something about her father's looming
financial troubles, and had decided to distance his family
from a potential scandal.

To widespread local astonishment, Sir Robert had announced his own early retirement, and the sale of his company to a European conglomerate. Following this, within a
few weeks of Alastair's departure, the Court had been
closed up, and the Markhams had gone to live in Spain.

'Joining the sangria set,' Mrs Hawkins the post mistress had remarked. 'She'll fit right in there.'

But now, it seemed, they were coming back, although that didn't necessarily mean that Alastair would be returning with them. That could be just wishful thinking on Jenny's part, she acknowledged.

And Chessie hadn't wanted to question her too closely about what she'd heard. For one thing, Jenny should not have been hanging round the post office eavesdropping on other people's conversations. For another, Chessie didn't want to give the impression she was too interested.

The burned child fears the fire, she thought wryly. She'd worn her heart on her sleeve once for Alastair already. This time, she would be more careful.

If there was a 'this time...'

'My God, Chessie, I'd hardly have known you.'

Was that what he'd say when—if—he saw her again?

Certainly, she bore little resemblance to the girl he'd known. The Chessie of that summer had had hair streaked with sunlight. Her honey-tanned skin had glowed with youth and health as well as happiness, and her hazel eyes had smiled with confidence at the world about her.

Now, she seemed like a tone poem in grey, she thought, picking at her unremarkable skirt and blouse. And it wasn't just her clothes. The reflection in the window looked drab—defeated.

Yet any kind of style or flamboyance had not seemed an option in those hideous weeks between her father's arrest for fraud and his fatal heart attack on remand.

She'd survived it all—the stories in the papers, the visits of the fraud squad, Jenny's descent into hysteria—by deliberately suppressing her identity and retreating behind a wall of anonymity. Something she'd maintained ever since.

She'd expected to find herself a kind of pariah, and yet, with a few exceptions, people in the village had been kind and tactful, making it easy for her to adopt this new muted version of her life.

And working for Miles Hunter had helped too, in some curious way. It had been a tough and exacting time with little opportunity for recriminations or brooding.

In the last few months, she'd even managed to reach some kind of emotional plateau just short of contentment.

Now, thanks to Jenny's news, she felt unsettled again.

She was about to turn back to her desk when she heard the sound of an engine. Craning her neck, she saw Miles Hunter's car sweep round the long curve of the drive and come to a halt in front of the main door.

A moment later, he emerged from the driver's seat. He stood for a moment, steadying himself, then reached for his cane and limped slowly towards the shallow flight of steps that led up to the door.

Chessie found she was biting her lip as she watched him. Her own current problems were just so minor compared to his, she thought, with a flicker of the compassion she'd never dared show since that first day she'd worked for him.

It was something she'd never forgotten—the way he'd stumbled slightly, getting out of his chair, and how, instinctively, she'd jumped up herself, her hands reaching out to him.

The blue eyes had been glacial, his whole face twisted in a snarl as he'd turned on her. 'Keep away. Don't touch me.'

'I'm so sorry.' She'd been stricken by the look, and the tone of his voice. 'I was just trying to help...'

'If I need it, I'll ask for it. And I certainly don't want pity. Remember that.'

She'd wanted to hand in her notice there and then, but she hadn't because she'd suddenly remembered a very different exchange.

'He had the world at his feet once,' Mr Jamieson, their family solicitor, had told her when he'd first mentioned the possibility of a job, and staying on at Silvertrees. 'Rugby blue—played squash for his county—award-winning journalist in newspaper and television. And then found himself in the wrong place at the wrong moment, when the convoy he was travelling with met a land-mine.'

He shook his head. 'His injuries were frightful. They thought he'd never walk again, and he had umpteen skin grafts. But while he was in hospital recovering, he wrote his first novel *The Bad Day*.'

'Since which, he's never looked back, of course.' Chessie spoke with a certain irony.

Mr Jamieson looked at her with quiet solemnity over the top of his glasses. 'Oh, no, my dear,' he said gently. 'I think it likely he looks back a good deal—don't you?'

And Francesca felt herself reproved.

She was back at her desk, working away, when Miles Hunter came in.

'I've just seen your sister,' he remarked without preamble. 'She nearly went into the car with that damned bike of hers. Doesn't it possess brakes?'

'Yes, of course,' Chessie said hurriedly, groaning inwardly. 'But she does ride it far too fast. I—I'll speak to her.'

Miles Hunter gave her a sardonic look. 'Will that do any good? She seems a law unto herself.'

'Well, I can try at least.'

'Hmm.' He gave her a considering look. 'She seemed stirred up about something, and so do you. Has she been upsetting you again?'

'Jenny does not upset me.' Chessie lifted her chin.

'Of course not,' he agreed affably, then sighed impatiently. 'Just who are you trying to fool, Francesca? You spend half your life making allowances for that girl—tiptoeing around her feelings as if you were treading on eggshells. I'm damned if she does half as much for you.'

Indignation warred inside her with shock that Miles Hunter, who invariably addressed her as Miss Lloyd, should suddenly have used her first name.

'It's been very difficult for her...' she began defensively.

'More than for you?'

'In some ways. You see, Jenny...' She realised she was about to say, Jenny was my father's favourite, but the words died on her lips. It was something she'd never admitted before, she realised, shocked. Something she'd never even allowed herself to examine. She found herself substituting lamely, 'Was very young when all this happened to us.'

'You don't think it's time she took on some responsibility for her own life, perhaps?' The dark face was quizzical.

'You're my employer, Mr Hunter,' Chessie said steadily. 'But that's all. You're not our guardian, and you have no right to judge. Jenny and I have a perfectly satisfactory relationship.'

'Well, she and I do not,' he said grimly. 'When I suggested, quite mildly, that she should look where she was going, she called back that soon I wouldn't have to bother about either of you. What did she mean by that?'

Chessie would have given a great deal to put her hands round Jenny's throat and choke her.

'I think perhaps you misheard her,' she said, cursing silently. 'What Jenny means is that she'll be going to university in the autumn and—'

'If her results are good enough.'

'There's no problem about that,' Chessie said stiffly. 'She's a very bright girl, and they expect her to do well.'

'Let's hope that their optimism is rewarded. I can't say that sharing a roof with her has been an unalloyed delight.'

Ouch. Chessie bit her lip. 'I'm sorry.'

'You haven't a thing to apologise for. You haven't the age or experience to cope with a temperamental adolescent. Wasn't there anyone else who could have helped?'

She wanted to tell him sharply that she didn't need help, thanks, but her intrinsic honesty prevailed. She said quietly, 'I have an aunt on my mother's side, but she didn't want her family involved—and who can blame her? Anyway, it doesn't matter.'

'Of course it matters,' he said. 'You're a human being, although you do your best, most of the time, to pretend you're some kind of robot.' He stopped abruptly. 'Oh, for God's sake, I didn't mean that.' He paused. 'Look, can I ask you something before I stumble into any more verbal disasters?'

'If you want.' *Robot*, she thought. *Grey robot*. That said it all.

'Would you have dinner with me this evening?'

For the first time in her life, Chessie felt her jaw drop. 'I—I don't understand.'

'It's quite simple. It may not seem like it, but I've had a really good day. My agent has actually sold *Maelstrom* to Evening Star Films, and they want me to write the first draft of the screenplay, so there's a slight chance of part of my original concept surviving.'

She saw his smile so seldom that she'd forgotten what a charge it could pack, lighting his whole face with charm, and turning his eyes to sapphire. Forcing her to startled acknowledgement of his attraction.

'I'd really like to celebrate,' he went on. 'And as *Maelstrom* was the first book you were involved with, I'd be honoured if you'd join me.'

She continued to stare at him.

Finally, he said, 'You do eat—don't you?'

'Yes—but...'

'But what?'

Chessie moved her hands defensively. 'It's a kind thought, but I don't think we should. After all, this is quite a small village.'

'I was asking you to dinner,' he said with studied patience. 'Not to bed. If you want, I'll put a notice to that effect in the parish magazine.'

Her face warmed. 'I'm sure you find it all very parochial and amusing,' she said. 'But I've managed to establish that ours is strictly a working relationship, which is important as we live under the same roof. If I'm seen having dinner with you, people might assume—things have changed. And that could embarrass both of us.'

And I've lived through one lot of gossip and scandal, she added silently. I don't relish the thought of any more.

'I really don't embarrass that easily.' He sounded amused. 'But I could always call in a builder, and have the communicating door between your flat and the rest of the house bricked up. That should silence the clacking tongues.'

'I'm trying to be serious,' she protested.

'And, for once, I'm trying to be frivolous, not with any conspicuous success,' he added drily. 'Can't you look on the invitation as an expression of gratitude—an additional bonus? Anyway—' he cast her a frowning but all-encompassing glance '—you look as if you could do with a square meal. You could rent out your collar-bones as salt-cellars.'

'Thank you,' Chessie said with something of a snap. 'But I don't think—'

'Precisely,' Miles interrupted flatly. 'Don't think. Do something on impulse for a change. It's only a meal, for heaven's sake.' He paused, his face hardening. 'Or do you find my physical appearance distressing? Because I can assure you all the worst scars are hidden.'

'*No.*' Her flush deepened. 'That's a terrible thing to imply.'

'It happens,' he returned. 'I was living with someone before the ill-fated assignment. We'd talked about marriage—made plans. When I came out of hospital and she saw me without my clothes for the first time, she didn't want to know any more.' He paused. 'And that is a matter of pure fact—not a plea for sympathy.'

'You've made it more than clear that sympathy is the last thing you want, Mr Hunter.' She hesitated. 'But I will have dinner with you—if that's what you want.'

'Thank you,' he said quietly. 'Do you think you could bend another rule, and call me Miles?'

Chessie felt suddenly confused. This, she thought, is not right, and I should put a stop to it, here and now.

Instead, she heard herself say awkwardly, 'Very well—Miles.'

He nodded gravely. 'Absolutely the right decision. I'll see you out by the car at eight.'

He limped across to the adjoining study and went in, closing the door behind him.

Chessie looked blankly at the computer. The screensaver had clicked on, and she was confronted by a series of coloured geometric patterns, endlessly changing shape as they whirled slowly in front of her.

I know, she thought, how they feel.

It was turning into a day for surprises, and she wasn't sure she cared for any of them. Particularly the latest one.

Had she really committed herself to going to dinner with Miles Hunter? she asked herself incredulously.

She thought, Well, it's too late to turn back now, and shivered as if she'd found herself on the edge of some nameless danger...

And that was a complete overreaction, she added flatly, probably brought on by reading too many thrillers by Miles Hunter. From now on, she'd switch to biographies about people who'd led very boring lives.

After all—and he'd said it himself—it was only a meal.

CHAPTER TWO

'THE Ogre's asked you out to dinner?' Jenny looked blank with disbelief. 'And you've actually accepted.' She shook her head. 'God, Chessie, you must be out of your tree.'

Chessie shrugged defensively. 'I don't see why. Something marvellous happened for him today, and he wants to celebrate.'

'Don't tell me,' Jenny said derisively. 'They've invented a mask for him to wear—like the Phantom of the Opera.'

Chessie stared at her, appalled. 'What an utterly foul thing to say,' she said slowly. 'Miles is my boss, and we owe him a great deal, yet you can't say one decent word to him, or about him.'

'Owe him?' Jenny's face reddened. 'What the hell do we owe him? He's taken our home away from us, and he's making us pay for it by treating us like drudges.'

'Really?' snapped Chessie. 'Well, I haven't noticed much drudgery from your direction. And if Miles hadn't bought this house, someone else would have done so, and we'd have been out on our ears. There was no way we could keep it. Why can't I get that through to you?'

Jenny looked mutinous. 'Well, I still think we could have done something. I saw this thing on television the other day about small country house hotels. It was really cool. I bet we could have made a bomb with Silvertrees.'

'In about twenty years, maybe,' Chessie said levelly. 'But Dad's creditors weren't prepared to wait that long for their money. And our present existence is like a holiday camp, compared with hotel-keeping. That's a twenty-four-hour job.'

Jenny sniffed. 'I still think it could have worked,' she said obstinately.

Chessie was suddenly caught between tears and laughter. Extraordinary how Jenny, so clever at school, could have such a tenuous hold on reality at other times.

She wondered what role her sister had pictured for herself in this make-believe ménage. Acting as receptionist, no doubt, and arranging a few flowers. Because she couldn't cook to save her life, and had never shown the slightest aptitude for housework either.

'And, anyway—' Jenny got down to the nitty-gritty of the situation '—if you're going out tonight, what am I going to eat? I bet The Ogre hasn't invited me.'

'No, he hasn't,' Chessie agreed. 'But you won't starve. There's some chicken casserole in the fridge. All you have to do is use the microwave.'

'Hardly on a level with being wined and dined.' Jenny pulled a face. 'And another thing—since when has The Ogre been "Miles" to you? I thought it was strictly, "Yes, Mr Hunter, sir."'

'So it was, and probably will be again tomorrow,' Chessie told her calmly. 'It's just a meal, that's all.'

I wonder how many times I'm going to say that before I convince even myself, she thought later as she reviewed the meagre contents of her wardrobe.

It had been a long time since she'd eaten in a restaurant. She'd been having lunch with her father, she remembered, hardly able to eat as she'd tried nervously to probe what had been going on in the company.

She could recall the uneasy questions she'd asked—the reassurances she'd sought.

Neville had patted her shoulder. 'Everything's going to be all right.' She could hear his voice now. 'There's nothing for my girl to worry about.'

He'd talked loudly, and laughed a lot. Drunk a lot too. He'd seen some former business associates across the restaurant, and had waved to them expansively, beckoning them over, but they hadn't come.

Even then that had seemed ominous, like the first crack in a dam, only she hadn't dared say so. Hadn't even wanted to acknowledge it could have been so. Longed for it all to have been her imagination.

She'd worn a plain cream linen shift, she remembered, with large gold buttons. That didn't exist any more, sadly, and she had little else that was suitable for dining out in.

Most of her clothes fell into two categories, she realised regretfully. There was working (ordinary) and working (slightly smarter). In the end, she opted for a plain black skirt reaching to mid-calf, and topped it with an ivory silk chainstore blouse. The gilt earrings and chains that Jenny had given her for her last birthday made the outfit seem a little more festive.

She was in her early twenties and she felt a hundred years old. There were little worry lines forming between her brows, and the curve of her mouth was beginning to look pinched.

She usually wore her light brown hair gathered for neatness into a rubber band at the nape of her neck, but decided to let it loose for once, its newly washed silkiness brushing her shoulders.

The only eye-shadow she possessed had formed into a sullen lump in the bottom of its little jar. Jenny had some make-up, she knew, purchased from her scanty and infrequent earnings delivering leaflets round the village, but, under the circumstances, a request for a loan would go down like a lead balloon, so she just used powder and her own dusky coral lipstick.

As a final touch, she unearthed her precious bottle of 'L'Air du Temps' from the back of her dressing-table drawer, and applied it to her throat and wrists. When it was gone, there would be no more, she thought, re-stoppering the bottle with care.

The salary she was paid was a good one, but there was little money left over for luxuries like scent.

Jenny had won a scholarship to the school in the neighbouring town where she was a day girl, so Chessie had no actual fees to find. But there was so much else. The only acceptable sports gear and trainers had to come with designer labels, and the school had a strict uniform code too, which had been a nightmare while Jenny was growing so rapidly.

But her sister was going to have exactly the same as all the other girls. She'd been determined about that from the first. No ridicule or snide remarks from her peers for Jenny.

But no one said it was easy, she thought, grimacing, as she picked up her all-purpose jacket and bag.

She paused to take a long critical look at herself in the mirror.

Did she really look the kind of girl a best-selling novelist would ask out? The answer to that was an unequivocal 'no', and she found herself wondering why he hadn't sought more congenial company.

Because, no matter what cruel comments Jenny might make, there was no doubt that Miles Hunter was an attractive and dynamic man, in spite of the scar on his face. And she wondered why it had taken her so long to realise this.

But then, she'd hardly regarded him in the light of a human being, she thought wryly. He was the man she worked for, and his initial rejection of her compassion had barred any personal rapport between them. He'd become a figurehead, she thought. A dark god who had to be constantly placated if she and Jenny were to survive.

She found herself thinking about the girl he'd told her about—the fiancée who'd ditched him because of his scars. Was he still embittered about this? Still carrying a torch for the woman who'd let him down when he'd most needed her support?

Could this be why, apart from the fan mail, which she dealt with herself, there were no phone calls or letters from women—apart from his sister, and his agent, who was in her late forties?

And could it also be why there was no love interest in his books—not the slightest leavening of romance?

He was a terrific writer, and the tension in his stories never slackened. Each book went straight into the best-seller lists after publication, yet if Chessie was honest she found his work oddly bleak, and even sterile.

But that's just my opinion, she told herself ruefully as she let herself out through the side door. The thriller-reading public who snapped him up had no such reservations.

Besides, she didn't know for sure that Miles had no women in his life. He was away a great deal in London, and other places. He could well be having a whole series of affairs without her being aware of it. Maybe he just liked to keep his personal life private—and away from the village.

He was waiting by the car. He was wearing beautifully cut casual trousers, which moulded his long legs, and a high-necked sweater in black cashmere. A sports jacket was slung across one shoulder.

He was staring at the ground, looking preoccupied and slightly cross, failing to notice her soft-footed approach.

He didn't seem to be looking forward to a pleasant evening, thought Chessie, wondering if he was regretting his impulsive invitation. If so, she was sure she would soon know, she told herself philosophically.

She found herself hoping that Jenny hadn't eaten the entire chicken casserole, because she might well be joining her.

She said, 'Good evening,' her voice shy and rather formal.

He looked up instantly, his eyes narrowing as if, for a moment, he had forgotten who she was. Then he nodded abruptly.

'Punctual as always,' he commented, opening the passenger door for her.

Well, what did he expect? Chessie wondered defensively as she struggled with her seat belt. She was hardly going to hang about coyly in the house, keeping him waiting.

As he joined her she caught a hint of his cologne, slightly musky and obviously expensive.

'I thought we'd try The White Hart,' Miles said as he started the engine. 'I hear the food's good there, if you don't mind the village pub.'

'Not at all.' Neither Chessie's clothes nor her confidence were up to a smart restaurant. 'Mrs Fewston's a marvellous cook. Before she and her husband took over the Hart, she used to cater for private dinner parties. In fact, I think she still does, sometimes.'

'I shall have to bear that in mind. It's time I did some entertaining.' He sent her a swift, sideways glance. 'Well, don't look so astonished. I can't go on accepting hospitality without returning it.'

'Er—no.' Chessie rallied. 'And Silvertrees is a great house for parties.'

'It's also a family house,' he said laconically. 'As my sister never fails to remind me.' He paused. 'I think that's a hint that I should invite her and her blasted kids to stay.'

'Don't you like children?'

He shrugged. 'I've never had much to do with them. Actually, Steffie's are great, although she calls them the monsters,' he added drily.

If it hadn't been for that land-mine, he might have been married with a family of his own by now, Chessie thought. She tried to imagine it, and failed.

But that was so unfair, she reproached herself. She was behaving just like Jenny. Because she'd never known the man he'd once been. The man who'd enjoyed everything life had to offer—who'd played sport, and laughed, and made love.

And the chances were she'd never have encountered him anyway.

Miles Hunter, the award-winning journalist and hard-hitting television reporter, would have been based in London. He wouldn't have been interested in a large, inconvenient house on the edge of a sleepy village. He'd have been where it was all happening—where he could pack a bag, and be off whenever a story broke.

He would probably never have contemplated becoming a novelist until circumstances had forced him to rethink his life completely.

Yet, here they both were. And together...

The White Hart was a pleasant timbered building, sited near the crossroads outside the village. A former coaching inn, it was always busy. Jim Fewston was as knowledgeable about wine as his wife was about cooking, and that kept the people coming. Tonight was no exception, and the car park was almost full when they arrived.

'Just as well I booked a table,' Miles commented as he slotted the car with expertise into one of the few available spaces. 'Although it would seem that not everyone's here for the food,' he added drily.

She followed his glance, and saw movement in a car parked on its own under the shelter of some trees. Glimpsed shadowy figures passionately entwined, and hurriedly looked away.

'What an odd place to choose.' She tried to match his tone.

'Not if you're having an illicit affair.' Miles shrugged. 'Presumably any corner will do.'

In the bar, Chessie drank an excellent dry sherry, and Miles a gin and tonic as they studied their menu cards.

Many of the people already there were local and known to her, and she'd been greeted cordially when she'd arrived, although a few of the greetings had been accompanied by slyly speculative glances.

But that was only to be expected, she thought as hunger drove out self-consciousness.

She chose watercress soup, and guinea fowl casseroled with shallots in red wine, while Miles opted for pâté, and steak cooked with Guinness and oysters.

'"Do you come here often?" is the usual opening gambit in this situation,' Miles commented sardonically as the waitress disappeared with their order. 'But I'm well aware that you don't, so what do you suggest as an alternative topic?'

'I'm not sure.' She played with the stem of her glass. 'I think my social graces are rusty with disuse.'

'And I doubt that I ever had any.' His mouth twisted in faint amusement. 'It promises to be a silent evening.'

'I'm quite used to that.' Tentatively, she returned his smile. 'Jenny spends most of her time in her room, studying for her exams, so I'm accustomed to my own company.'

'People tell me solitude is a luxury,' Miles said after a pause. 'But I'm not sure it works so well as a way of life.' He paused. 'What's your sister planning to do when she leaves school?'

'She's applied to read natural sciences, but I don't think she has any definite ideas about an ultimate career yet.' She thought she detected a faintly quizzical expression in the blue eyes, and hurried on defensively. 'But it's early days, and she doesn't have to make any hasty decisions.'

She leaned back against the comfortable red plush of the bench seat. 'I had to struggle every inch of the way at school, but learning seems to come easily to Jenny.'

'I'm glad to hear it,' Miles said politely, after another pause. 'There's a good St Emilion on the wine list, or would you prefer Burgundy?'

'No, the Bordeaux would be fine.' She remembered with a pang a holiday she'd once spent with her father, exploring the vineyards of south-west France. It had been a magical time for her, even though he'd constantly fussed about

Jenny left behind with her aunt's family, and made a point of phoning her each evening.

'There it is again,' Miles said quietly, and she looked at him in startled question.

'I'm sorry?'

'That expression of yours—like a child who's just heard Christmas has been abolished.'

'Oh, dear.' Chessie pantomimed dismay. 'How wimpish. I'll try and look more cheerful from now on.'

'Are all your memories so painful?'

She gave the pale liquid in her glass a fierce and concentrated stare. 'How did you know I was—remembering?'

'An educated guess—having attended the same school myself.' He finished his gin and tonic. 'Want to talk about it?'

She shook her head. 'What can anyone say? One minute you're riding high. The next, you're flat on your face in the mud, not knowing whether you'll ever get up again. That's my personal angle. The rest I'm sure you read in the newspapers at the time. They didn't leave many stones unturned.'

He said gently, 'It would have been difficult to miss.' He watched her for a moment. 'Well—aren't you going to say it?'

'Say what?'

'That your father was entirely innocent, and, but for his untimely death, he'd have cleared himself of all charges.'

Chessie slowly shook her head. She said bleakly, 'If he'd lived, I think he would still have been in jail. In many ways, his death was a mercy for him. He'd have hated—hated...'

She stopped, biting her lip. 'I'm sorry. I'm being very boring. This is supposed to be a celebration, not a wake.'

He said quietly, 'I would not have asked if I hadn't wanted to know, Francesca.'

But why did he want to know? she wondered as she drank some more sherry. Now that they were out of their working environment, maybe he felt he had to make conversation that didn't concern the current script or the purely domestic details either.

Yet he could have picked something less personal. Music, maybe, or cinema.

What did a man and a woman talk to each other about over dinner and a bottle of wine? She was so totally out of touch. And nervous.

She hadn't had a serious boyfriend since Alastair. The dates she'd gone out on in London had been totally casual and uncommitted. She couldn't think of one man out of all of them she'd wanted to see again, let alone know better.

And since London, of course, there'd been no one at all.

Until tonight—which naturally didn't count, she reminded herself swiftly.

It was a relief when the waitress came to say their table was ready. The soup and pâté, when they arrived, were so good that it was really only necessary to make appreciative noises and eat.

So Chessie made appreciative noises, and ate.

She and Miles had been put in one of the smaller rooms off the main dining room. It was panelled and candlelit, and intimate, with all the tables set for two. Even the flower arrangements were small, presumably to allow diners to gaze unimpeded into each other's eyes.

The Fewstons must have a romantic streak, Chessie thought, buttering her bread roll, still warm from the oven. But it had led them severely astray this time.

She'd have settled for a wall of delphiniums and hollyhocks to shelter behind. Or even a privet hedge.

While their plates were being changed, Chessie hurried into speech, asking about the film script, and what would be involved in adapting the book.

It wasn't just an excuse to find an impersonal topic, she told herself. She was genuinely interested, and after all she was going to be closely involved in the project.

But what next? The weather? Would it be a hot summer, and was it really the greenhouse effect?

Brilliant, she thought. *What a conversational ball of fire you are, Chessie, my dear.*

'Am I really such a difficult companion?' Miles leaned back in his chair, the blue eyes hooded.

Rocked back on her heels, Chessie took a gulp of wine, feeling her face warm with sudden colour.

'No, of course not,' she managed. *Although he could be a mind-reader.*

'Perhaps I should have told you to bring a notebook, and dictated a few letters between courses,' he went on. 'You might have felt more at ease then.'

'I doubt it.' She put down her glass. 'I still don't understand what I'm doing here.'

'You're eating an excellent meal,' he said. 'Which you haven't had to prepare, cook, and wash up after.'

'And that's all there is to it?' She felt oddly breathless.

'No, but the rest can wait.' The cool face was enigmatic, the scar silver in the candlelight. 'May I refill your glass?'

'I don't think so.' Chessie covered it with a protective hand. 'Something tells me I need to keep a clear head.'

His smile mocked her. 'I haven't seduction in mind, if that's what you're thinking.'

'It never crossed my mind.'

'How incredibly pure of you,' he murmured. 'Considering the amount of time we spend alone together, have you really never wondered why I've never made a pass at you? Or do you think my scars have rendered me immune from the normal male urges?'

She bit her lip. 'I don't suppose that for a moment. But I took it for granted that passes were out because of our situation—the terms of my employment. And because...' She paused.

'Yes?' Miles prompted.

She swallowed. 'Because it would be—inappropriate behaviour, and tacky as well. The amorous boss and his secretary—that's a cliché, and you don't deal in clichés,' she added in a rush.

'Thank you—I think,' he remarked sardonically. 'Yet it was our—situation that I wanted to discuss with you.'

'Have you decided to sell the house?' Her last exquisite mouthful of guinea fowl turned to ashes in her mouth. Suddenly she was contemplating the prospect of being homeless and back on the job market at the same time.

It had always been a possibility, she supposed, yet just lately—stupidly—she'd allowed herself to feel settled. Safe even.

'Absolutely not.' He looked genuinely surprised. 'What gave you that idea? Didn't you hear me say I was planning to do some entertaining?'

'Yes—I'm sorry.' She hesitated. 'I suppose insecurity makes you paranoid.'

'I can appreciate that.' He put down his knife and fork, frowning slightly. 'That's part of the reason I want you to consider a change in your terms of employment.'

'A change?' Chessie was puzzled. Her contract with Miles had been carefully and meticulously defined. There were no obvious loopholes or room for manoeuvre. 'What kind of change?'

He drank some more wine, the blue eyes meditative as he studied her across the top of the glass.

He said, 'I thought we might get married.'

Chessie had a curious feeling that the entire world had come to a sudden halt, throwing her sideways. The subdued hum of conversation and laughter around them faded under the swift roar of blood in her ears.

Her whole body was rigid as she stared at him, lips parted in astonishment as she tried to make sense of what he'd just said.

'I'm sorry,' she said at last in a voice that seemed to have travelled vast distances across space and time. 'I don't think I quite understand.'

'It's perfectly simple. I've just proposed to you—asked you to become my wife.' He sounded totally cool about it—unbelievably matter-of-fact. 'Look on it, if you want, as a new kind of contract.'

He was mad, she thought dazedly. That was the answer. Completely and totally insane. Suffering some kind of delayed shell-shock.

Her lips moved. 'Marriage is—hardly a business arrangement.'

'I'd say that depends on the people involved.' His gaze was steady. 'Considering our individual circumstances and problems, marriage between us seems a sensible idea.'

He paused. 'You need more stability and security than you currently enjoy, and I'm going to require a hostess as well as a housekeeper. I think we could work out a perfectly satisfactory deal.'

'Just like that?' Her voice sounded faint. She still could not believe what was happening.

'No, of course not,' he said with a trace of impatience. 'I don't want an immediate answer. But I'd like you to give my proposal some coherent and rational thought before you reach any decision.'

Coherent? she thought. Rational—when applied to *this*? The words were meaningless.

'Judging by your reaction, this has been a bit of a thunderbolt,' he went on.

'Yes.' Chessie swallowed. 'You—could say that.' She spread her hands in an almost pleading gesture. 'I mean— we hardly know each other.'

'We work together every day, and we live in the same house. That's not exactly a casual acquaintance.'

'Yes—but…' She fought for the right words, and lost. 'Oh, you know exactly what I mean.'

'I think so.' His face was sardonic. 'You're still pondering the lack of amorous advances.'

'It's not that—or not totally, anyway.' She pushed her glass at him. 'I will have some more wine, please. I seem to need it.'

She watched him pour, his hand steady. He was completely calm, she thought incredulously. Detached, even. But how could that be, when he'd just turned her world upside down?

She hurried into speech again. 'There's never been anything remotely personal between us—not until now. Yes, we've seen each other every day, but we've never talked about anything but work, and problems to do with the house.' Mostly created by Jenny, she realised with a pang. Then—oh, God—Jenny.

'Has this shift in our relationship plunged you into some kind of trauma?' he drawled. 'I didn't intend that.'

'No—but it's all so sudden.' She stopped, grimacing. 'Hell, now I sound like the heroine of a bad historical novel.'

'And highly sensible of the honour I've just done you.' It was his turn to pull a face. 'Only I don't think you are, by any means. You look more winded than appreciative.'

'Being hit by a thunderbolt doesn't usually call for appreciation,' Chessie said with something of a snap. 'What did you expect—that I'd fall into your arms?'

'Hardly. You'd damage the crockery.' He was silent for a moment. 'If you're saying you'd have preferred a conventional courtship, then I can only apologise. But we've always had a reasonable working relationship, and our marriage would simply be an extension of this. So I thought the pragmatic approach would have more credence than hearts and flowers.'

Chessie said with difficulty, 'It doesn't—worry you that we're not in love with each other?'

'You forget I've been down that path once already. I can't speak for you, of course.' His face was expressionless. 'Is there anyone?'

She shook her head. 'No—not any more.' She kept her eyes fixed on the tablecloth. 'So it would be just a business arrangement—not a real marriage at all.'

'Yes,' he said. 'Initially, anyway.'

Her heart thudded in renewed shock. 'But later...?'

He shrugged. 'Who knows?' The blue eyes met hers directly. 'Ultimately, we might think again.' He paused. 'But any alteration in the terms would only be by mutual agreement.'

'I—I don't know what to say.'

'Then say nothing. Not yet. Just think about it, and take as long as you need. I promise I won't pressure you.'

She flicked the tip of her tongue round dry lips. 'And if I decide—no? Will I find myself out of a job?'

'Do I seem that vindictive?'

She reddened. 'No—no, of course not.' She took a deep breath. 'Very well. I'll—consider it.'

'Good.' His smile was swift, without a trace of mockery this time. 'Now shall I tell them to bring the dessert menu?'

'No, thanks.' Chessie doubted whether she could force another mouthful of food past her taut throat muscles. She pushed back her chair. 'Just coffee, please. And will you excuse me?'

The ladies' cloakroom was fortunately deserted. Chessie ran cool water over her wrists in a vain effort to quieten her hammering pulses.

She didn't look like someone who'd just been poleaxed, she thought, staring at her reflection, although her eyes were enormous, and there was more colour in her cheeks than usual.

But nor did she look like the future wife of Miles Hunter.

But then she wasn't really going to be a wife at all, she reminded herself, absently sifting her fingers through the bowl of pot pourri on the vanity unit, and savouring its fragrance.

Her present duties were being extended—that was all. Her change of status would permit her to sit at the opposite end of that beautiful oak dining table when there were guests, but little more.

She supposed he would expect her to move out of the flat, and live in the main house again.

She might even get her old bedroom back—for a while.

Initially. That was the word he'd used. But he'd also said *'ultimately'*, she thought, her heart beginning to pound unevenly. And what then?

She was shaking all over suddenly, her mind closing off in startled rejection.

'I can't,' she whispered. 'I couldn't. I'll have to tell him here and now that it's impossible.'

But she'd promised to consider his proposal, and she'd have to pretend to do so at least.

But she could not marry him. Not in a million years. Not even if Alastair never came back...

Chessie drew a deep, trembling sigh. There—she'd faced it at last. She'd allowed herself to admit the existence of the dream—the little foolish, groundless hope that had been growing inside her ever since she'd heard Jenny's news.

And how ironic that Miles should have chosen today of all days to present her with his own plan for her future.

'It never rains but it pours.' That was what Mrs Chubb, their current and longest-serving daily help would say.

Her little laugh turned into a groan. Once she'd told Miles her decision, it would be impossible for her to stay on at Silvertrees. In spite of his assurances, it would make things altogether too awkward.

There was a temping agency in the nearby town. She would make enquiries there, and then trawl through the letting bureaux for the cheapest possible flat.

Oh, *why* had Miles done this to her? she asked herself with something bordering on despair. Things had been fine as they were, and now everything was ruined again. And it wasn't as if he even *wanted* her.

Although that was something to be grateful for, at least. Because what would she have done if he had ever made a move on her?

Before she could stop herself, for one startled, stunned moment, she found she was imagining herself in Miles' arms, breathing the musky scent of his skin, feeling his mouth move on hers, coaxing her lips apart. His lean, long-fingered hand grazing her skin in a first caress...

Chessie came gasping back to reality, like a diver reaching the surface of some deep lake. Every inch of her body was tingling. Inside the silk shirt, her small breasts were burning, the nipples hardening helplessly.

Her eyes were green, like a drowsy cat's, she thought, gazing at herself in horror. Her lips, parted and trembling.

There was no way she could return to the table like this. Or he would know. And then she would be totally lost.

Oh, God, she thought frantically. What's happening to me? And what am I doing to myself?

And could find no answer that made any sense at all.

CHAPTER THREE

IF I don't go back to the table soon, thought Chessie, comb-ing her hair for the umpteenth time, Miles will be sending out a search party.

Her skin no longer scorched her, but she was still shaking inside, and her hand felt too unsteady to renew her lipstick.

The cloakroom door opened, and two girls came in, gig-gling together. Chessie was aware of the curious glances they sent her as they passed by.

She thought, I cannot go on hiding like this.

As she walked reluctantly back towards the dining area, she was waylaid by Jim Fewston. 'Evening, Miss Lloyd. Hope you enjoyed your meal.'

'The food was delicious,' she assured him. *But as for enjoyment...*

'And how's that young sister of yours?' He shook his head. 'These days—they grow up before you know it.'

'Yes,' Chessie said. 'I suppose they do.'

'Sometimes,' he went on. 'they can be a little too grown-up for their own good.'

Suddenly, Chessie was uneasy. Up to then she'd thought Mr Fewston was just being the jovial landlord. Now, she wasn't so sure.

He lowered his voice confidentially. 'I hope she wasn't too put out the other night. In a strange pub, she might have got away with it, but I've known her all her life, as you might say, and I know she's not eighteen yet.'

He paused. 'The local police are down on under-age drinking like a ton of bricks, and I'm not prepared to risk my licence. I don't care for the lad she was with either, so when she started pushing her luck, and asking for vodka and tonic, I had to ask them to leave.'

He sighed. 'I'm sure you understand my position, and no hard feelings either way.'

'I don't think I understand much at all.' Chessie shook her head. 'Are you saying that Jenny has been in here trying to buy alcohol? I'm sorry, but you must be mistaken.'

'No mistake, Miss Lloyd.' His voice was kind, but firm. 'Why don't you ask her, my dear? Often a quiet word is all that's needed. I know it can't be easy raising a girl of that age when you're only a slip of a thing yourself, but this is something that wants nipping in the bud. And I'd keep an eye on her boyfriends, too,' he added with a touch of grimness.

'But Jenny has no boyfriends.' Chessie's protest was bewildered. 'She doesn't even go out at night. She's in her room, studying.'

'Not every night, Miss Lloyd, and other publicans will tell you the same. I suggest you make enquiries.' He gave her a polite nod, and went back into the bar.

She stood for a moment, staring after him dazedly, trying to assimilate what he'd told her. To make some sense of it. Jenny, she thought. *Jenny?*

As she made her way back to the table she saw that their waitress had brought the cafetière. But she didn't move away immediately. She was smiling and talking as she rearranged the cups and cream jug, bending over the table towards Miles as she did so. Fiddling with the collar of her blouse, Chessie realised, and pushing back her hair.

My God, she thought incredulously. She's coming on to him. She really is. And he's not exactly brushing her off either. He's leaning back in his chair, amused, but taking the whole thing in his stride.

It brought home to her once again just how little she really knew about the way in which Miles Hunter conducted his private life. In fact the entire evening had awoken all kinds of uncertainties she could well have done without.

She found herself moving forward more quickly, and the girl, noticing her approach, gave one last smile then hurried away.

As Chessie sank into her seat Miles glanced across at her, his brows snapping together interrogatively. 'What's wrong?'

'Not a thing.' Chessie summoned a smile of her own. 'I was just thinking how attentive the service is here.' She could hear the waspishness in her voice, and groaned inwardly. The last thing she wanted was to sound jealous or proprietorial in any way.

But Miles, fortunately, seemed oblivious to any undercurrents.

'Your friends run a smooth operation,' he returned. 'But that doesn't alter the fact that there's something the matter. What is it? Are you ill?'

'No—really.' She swallowed. 'But it's getting late. Would you mind if we just paid the bill and left?'

'Yes, I think I would,' he said unexpectedly. 'Whatever Jenny's been up to, it can wait until we've completed our first meal together in a civilised manner. In fact, I suggest you have a brandy. You look as if you need it.'

Indignation swamped her. 'Why should it be anything to do with Jenny?'

'Because that's what that stricken look of yours inevitably means.' His glance challenged her to deny it. 'Will you have that brandy?'

Biting her lip, she nodded silently.

'Good.' Miles gave her a faint smile as he signalled to the waitress. 'Rushing off in all directions won't solve a thing.'

'It's so easy for you,' she said bitterly. 'Jenny is not your responsibility.'

'Not at the moment, certainly.' He saw the swift colour flood her face, and his smile widened sardonically. 'Which,

I suppose, is your cue to tell me that you wouldn't have me if I came gift-wrapped.'

'No.' She didn't look at him. 'You asked me to think it over, and I will.' After all, she reasoned, she needed a breathing space to find a new job—a new flat. And she needn't feel too badly about it either. Judging by tonight's performance, he'd have little trouble finding a replacement when she turned him down.

'Hopefully it will have the added bonus of diverting your mind from Jenny, too.' He paused. 'I suppose you've discovered she isn't the saintly, single-minded scholar you took her for.'

'School used to mean everything to her.' Her voice was tired.

'I expect it did—while she was healing. It was safety—security, and she could use her studies to block out what was going on in the real world.' Miles shrugged. 'But the young recover fast, and now she's ready to rebel.'

He leaned forward. 'Face it, Francesca. Jenny's bright, but she's also spoiled, and brimming with resentment. Something had to give.' He smiled brief thanks at the blushing waitress as she put Chessie's brandy on the table, then reached for the cafetière. 'Cream and sugar?'

'Just black.' Desolation had her by the throat. 'I've failed her, haven't I?'

'Of course not. But you're not experienced enough to see the warning signs, and impose sanctions in time.' He handed over her cup. 'So, instead of revising, she was cavorting round the neighbourhood, right?'

'Apparently. The light was on in her room, and she used to play music all the time.' Chessie shook her head. 'It never occurred to me to check she was actually there. And, all the time, she was out, trying to con vodka and tonics out of unsuspecting landlords. With some fellow that Jim Fewston doesn't approve of.'

Miles raised his eyebrows. 'At least she's not drinking alone. It could be worse.'

She gave a small, wintry smile. 'I think it's about as bad as it gets.'

'Then you're being naïve.' He spoke gently. 'But I do understand that you need to see Jenny and talk to her about it, so, as soon as we've drunk our coffee, I'll take you home.'

'Thank you.' Her voice was subdued. 'I—I'm sorry that I've spoiled your celebration.'

'I promise that you haven't spoiled a thing.' He smiled at her. 'On the contrary.'

He thought she was going to accept his proposal, Chessie realised as she drank her coffee. And, on the face of it, she had every reason to do so. Marrying Miles would provide her with the kind of security she could dream about otherwise.

He obviously saw it as a practical solution to both their problems. The same cold-blooded approach he brought to his novels, she thought bitterly. And although you were swept along by the sheer force of the action, you were invariably left feeling slightly cheated at the end.

But I can't cheat him, she thought, swallowing. And I won't cheat myself either. We both deserve better from life. And we don't have to settle for second-best, just because we're both still hung up on other people.

She studied him covertly under her lashes, wondering what the girl he'd loved had been like. Attractive, if not actually beautiful, that was certain. A trail-blazer, probably, bright and sharp, with bags of energy, sexual as well as emotional. And demanding high standards in every aspect of her life, including the physical attraction of the man she'd chosen to share it. But ruthless when he'd failed to satisfy her criteria.

She jumped, startled, when he said softly, 'You're looking bereft again. I think we'd better go.'

While he was at the cash desk, dealing with the bill, Chessie wandered out into the reception area, and stood

looking without seeing at the display of watercolour land-
scapes by local artists that were featured there.

It was the sudden wave of fragrance in the air—half forgotten, but haunting—commingling the scent of some
heavy sweet perfume and Sobranie cigarettes that alerted
her to the fact that she was no longer alone. And that the
newcomer was known to her.

She half turned, arranging her face into polite pleasure,
expecting to greet an acquaintance, and stopped dead, staring with incredulity at the woman framed in the archway
that led to the bar.

She was eye-catching enough, her lush figure wrapped
in a silky leopard-skin print dress, and a black pashmina
thrown carelessly over her arm.

Violet eyes under extravagantly darkened lashes swept
Chessie from head to toe in an inspection bordering on
insolence. Full red lips parted in a smile that combined
mockery with a hint of malice.

'Well, well,' Linnet Markham said softly. 'If it isn't the
little Francesca. Now, who *would* have thought it?'

'Lady Markham.' Chessie swallowed. 'Linnet. So you're
back.'

'Don't sound so surprised,' Linnet drawled. 'I'm sure the
local grapevine has been working overtime.' She strolled
forward. 'But I'm astonished to find that you're still around.
I'd expected you to have made a fresh start somewhere a
long way from here—where you're not known.'

Chessie flushed. 'Fortunately not everyone agrees with
you. And I needed to provide stability for my sister.'

'Ah, yes.' Linnet said reflectively. 'The sister. She was
the pretty one, if my memory serves.'

'Indeed,' Chessie agreed quietly. 'And with brains, too.
In fact, you'd hardly credit that we were related.' She
paused. 'Is Sir Robert here with you?'

Linnet's smile developed a slight rigidity. 'No, he's still
in London. I came down ahead to oversee arrangements at
the house. You simply can't rely on staff,' she added, dis-

missing the faithful Mrs Cummings with a wave of her hand. 'I've booked into a hotel for a couple of nights. I just popped into the Hart for a drink for old times' sake.'

'I didn't realise it was a place you visited.'

Linnet shrugged. 'Oh, it's always been a good place to see people, and be seen.' She paused. 'But I'd have thought it way above your means,' she added, eyeing Chessie's blouse and skirt. 'Or are you working here as a waitress? You never really trained for much, did you? And you wouldn't have any real references either—working for your father.' Her brow furrowed. 'Nor anywhere decent to live. I presume Silvertrees House had to be sold.'

This, Chessie thought detachedly, was quite definitely the evening from hell. She lifted her chin. 'Yes, of course, but I happen to work for the new owner, and we still live there. I keep house for him, and do his secretarial work.'

'Well, that sounds a cosy little arrangement,' Linnet purred. 'You've certainly fallen on your feet. So, who is this paragon who's taken you on?'

Chessie hesitated. 'I work for Miles Hunter, the thriller writer,' she said reluctantly.

'Hunter?' The violet eyes sharpened. 'But he's a best-seller, isn't he? You see his books everywhere. He must be worth an absolute fortune.'

'He's very successful,' Chessie agreed, wincing inwardly at the older woman's crudity.

'And charitable to waifs and strays too, it seems.' Linnet's voice was cream spiced with acid. 'How did you manage it?'

Chessie shrugged, trying to control the temper boiling up inside her.

'He needed someone to run things for him,' she returned shortly. 'I was available.'

'I'm sure you were.' Linnet gave a small, tinkling laugh. 'However, I don't advise you to start getting any foolish ideas this time. No girlie crushes. Because not everyone's as understanding as Alastair.'

Chessie felt her whole body jolt with shock as if she'd been physically struck. Her nails curled into the palms of her hands. Over Linnet's shoulder, she saw Miles emerging from the dining room, pausing to lean on his cane as he slotted his wallet back into his jacket.

She said, 'Thanks for the warning, Linnet, but it really isn't necessary.'

She went to Miles, sliding her arm through his with deliberate possessiveness, and giving him a radiant smile.

'Darling, may I introduce Lady Markham, who's just come back to live at Wenmore Court? Linnet, this is Miles Hunter.' She paused quite deliberately. 'My fiancé.'

Miles did not move, but the sudden tension in his body hit her like an electric charge.

Later she would hate herself, and she knew it, but now the expressions chasing themselves across Linnet's face made it all worthwhile. Or nearly.

Linnet, however, made a lightning recovery. 'Congratulations.' She held out her hand to Miles, along with a smile that lingered appraisingly, and frankly approved.

My God, Chessie thought bleakly. First the waitress, now Linnet. Am I the only woman in Britain not to have registered his attraction on some personal Richter scale?

'So, when did all this happen?' Linnet went on.

'Tonight,' Miles returned, his face impassive. 'We've been having a celebratory dinner. You're the first to know.'

'How marvellous,' Linnet approved fulsomely. 'I'm sure you'll both be fabulously happy.' She paused. 'When's the big day? I suppose you'll marry locally?'

'We haven't decided yet,' Chessie intervened hastily. 'Miles has a book to finish, and a film deal, so he's incredibly busy just now.'

'How very unromantic you make me sound, my darling,' Miles said lightly. 'Actually, I think we should be married as soon as possible, although the honeymoon might have to wait for a while.'

He drew Chessie closer. Allowed his lips to graze her

hair. He said softly, 'I think it's time we went, don't you? So we can continue our celebration at home.'

Helpless colour warmed her face. She murmured something unintelligible, and moved forward, her arm still trapped in his.

He turned to Linnet, smiling. 'Goodnight, Lady Markham. It's been a pleasure. I hope we meet again soon.'

'Oh…' Linnet sent him a blinding look under her lashes '…you can count on that.'

They walked to the car in a silence that Chessie dared not break. Miles opened the passenger door for her, and she shot in like a fugitive seeking sanctuary.

He took his place beside her, and sat for a moment, staring straight ahead into the darkness.

Eventually, he said quietly, 'I take it that was a matter of expediency rather than a final answer.' He turned his head and looked at her. 'Well?'

Chessie bent her head, pressing her hands to her burning face. 'God, I'm so sorry,' she mumbled. 'That was a dreadful—an appalling thing to do. I—I don't know what you must think.'

'I think you needed to score points.' His voice was dry. 'And I can understand that, even if I don't applaud the means you employed.'

Chessie's voice shook. 'She thought I was a bloody waitress.'

'I doubt that very much,' he said sardonically. 'As you commented, the staff were attentive to a fault. Too much so, perhaps. No one could ever say that about you.'

Oh, *hell*, thought Chessie dismally. He knew exactly what I was getting at. And I want to die.

After a brief silence, he went on levelly, 'However, thanks to Lady Markham's intervention, we are now to all intents and purposes engaged to each other, and we'll behave accordingly.'

'Must we?' She stared at him beseechingly.

'Of course.' His scar looked silver in the moonlight.

Carved from stone. 'Any kind of volte-face at this stage would simply make us both look ridiculous, and I won't permit that.'

'Thank you.' Her voice quivered. 'You—you're very kind.'

He said quietly, 'Don't kid yourself, Francesca. At this moment, I feel a number of things, and kindness, believe me, is not one of them. Now I'll take you home.'

They completed the journey in another, to Chessie, unnerving silence.

Miles brought the car smoothly to a halt beside the flight of steps that led up to the housekeeper's flat.

Hunched in her seat, Chessie was aware that he'd turned his head, and was studying her.

Oh, what now? she thought, her skin tingling in sudden apprehension. And if he—reached for her, what would she do? How should she react? In the space of a few hours, her entire life had shifted on its axis, and she was floundering.

Instead: 'Would you like me to come in with you?' The offer was polite, no more. And he didn't move an inch.

She shook her head, weak with relief. 'I think it's better if I deal with this on my own. But—thank you, anyway,' she added stiltedly.

'One day, I'll have to teach you to show your gratitude more positively,' he murmured. 'Goodnight, Francesca. I'm sorry the evening was such a disaster for you. I'll see you in the morning.'

She stood in the moonlight, watching him drive away to the front of the house. He might have proposed marriage, but the protocol between boss and employee was still being maintained, she thought as she went slowly up the steps. Not that she'd have it any other way, of course.

She sighed, and switched her attention resolutely to her most immediate problem.

She had no idea what she was going to say to Jenny, or even how to approach the problem, although she could possibly begin with a pointed reference to the cost of electricity, she thought as she stepped into the narrow hall to find lights blazing everywhere.

As she took off her jacket the sitting-room door opened, and Jenny appeared wreathed in smiles. 'Chessie—at last. I've got the most wonderful surprise for you.'

'I think I've had all the surprises I can handle for one day,' Chessie told her grimly. 'We need to talk, young lady.'

'Oh, that can wait,' Jenny said in gleeful dismissal, and stood aside so that Chessie could precede her into the sitting room.

For a moment the whole world seemed to stop as she stared in total disbelief at the tall figure rising from the sofa to greet her.

Her heart lurched painfully. Her voice was barely a shaky whisper as she said, 'Alastair…?'

'No one else.' He walked across to her, and put his hands on her shoulders, smiling down into her startled eyes. 'Aren't you going to say "Welcome home"?'

'Yes—yes, of course.' She drew a deep, steadying breath. 'It—it's great to see you again. I just didn't expect…'

His look was quizzical. 'It can't be that much of a shock. Jenny says she told you we were reopening the Court.'

'Yes,' she said. 'Yes, she did.'

'And anyway…' his voice sank to a whisper '…you knew I'd be back one day—didn't you?'

No, she thought, with an odd detachment. I knew nothing of the sort. You disappeared from my life, and it felt like for ever.

She said, 'I—I assumed you'd decided to stay in America.'

'Well, it was tempting,' he conceded. 'And I wasn't short of offers. But when this merchant bank in the City came up with a job, it seemed too good to turn down. So, here I am.'

His smile widened. 'And aren't you the tiniest bit pleased to see me?'

'Of course I am.'

It was like Christmas, she thought, and her birthday. And having her most private and secret dream miraculously come true. But, like all dreams, there was still that touch of unreality about the whole thing—almost like a warning.

'Then show me,' he whispered, and bent his head to kiss her. But her body felt rigid in his arms, and her lips were numb, unresponsive as he tried to coax them apart.

'Is that all the welcome I get?' He sounded amused and slightly irritated at the same time as he let her go.

'I think I'm still in shock.' She tried to smile. 'How did you know where to find me—us?'

'I dropped my stuff off at the house,' he said. 'And Joyce Cummings filled me in on everything that's happened. With Jenny supplying the details, of course.'

'I can imagine,' Chessie said ruefully. She looked round. 'Where is she, anyway?'

'A tactful withdrawal, I'd guess, on the pretext of making more coffee.'

There were used cups on the fireside table, she saw, and a half-empty bottle of wine and two glasses. Her brows drew together.

'So I rush to your side,' Alastair went on. 'Only to find you're out, sampling the bright lights with your boss. Except Jenny made it sound like an act of charity. She tells me the guy's hideous with a disposition to match.'

Chessie bit her lip. 'Jenny could do with employing a little charity herself.'

'Oh, come on, love. You can hardly expect her to enjoy the situation. It's a hell of a comedown, after all.'

He paused. 'But never mind all that. This is hardly the reception I was anticipating.'

He sounded almost reproachful, she realised. He'd been expecting her to fall ecstatically into his arms—and why wasn't she doing exactly that? Because she'd imagined this moment—had longed for it so often. Had cried into her pillow as she'd wondered where he'd been, and what he'd been doing, and if he'd ever thought of her. And now he was here and she felt—blank.

She stepped backwards, shrugging off her jacket and tossing it across the arm of the sofa. 'Alastair, be reasonable. You disappear from our lives for years on end, then walk in, expecting everything to be just the same. Only, it doesn't work like that.' She couldn't believe how cool she sounded. How controlled.

'Are you cross with me because I didn't keep in touch?' His smile reached to her, coaxed her. 'I blame myself totally, believe me. But it's not easy from that distance. And I've never been much of a letter writer.'

There are telephones, Chessie thought. There is email. If I'd been the one to leave, I'd have kept the relationship going somehow.

'No,' she said. 'I appreciate that. And life has a habit of moving on.'

'But I'm back now,' he went on eagerly. 'And I'll make up for everything.' He shook his head remorsefully. 'Poor sweet, what a terrible time you've had. And having to live here, little better than a servant. It must be a nightmare.'

'Don't believe all Jenny's sob stories,' Chessie said quietly. 'The situation has its plus side as well.' She paused. 'I saw your stepmother earlier. She was in The White Hart having a drink.'

There was a small, odd silence, then he said, 'Yes, I gathered she was planning a visit. I'd hoped to get on with the alterations at the Court without interference.'

'Alterations?'

'Nothing too drastic.' He shrugged. 'We'll be converting a couple of the downstairs rooms in the West Wing—installing ramps—that kind of thing.'

Chessie frowned. 'I don't understand...'

'Didn't Linnet tell you—about my father?'

'She simply said he was still in London.'

'That's perfectly true,' Alastair said stonily. 'Out of sight, out of mind, apparently. She might also have mentioned he's in a private clinic, having tests after a stroke.'

Chessie gasped. 'Oh, Alastair, no. How dreadful. When did it happen?'

'A few weeks ago while they were still in Spain.' His face was hard. 'He was flown home five days ago. There's some paralysis, so he'll have to use a wheelchair for a while, and his speech has been affected, but the doctors are optimistic. They think he could recover well with therapy and proper care.' He was silent for a moment. 'I just hope that's true.'

'Oh, dear God.' Chessie remembered Sir Robert's tall, robust presence, his brisk stride, and the commanding power of his voice. She couldn't imagine him sick—diminished in any way. 'I'm so sorry.' She hesitated. 'In a way, it's fortunate you decided to take this job in London.'

'Yes, I suppose so.' He gave a brief, almost bitter sigh. 'Hell, what a mess.'

'But why didn't Linnet mention it to me?'

'Who knows why Linnet does anything?' Alastair said with a slight snap. 'After all, it's hardly something that can be kept under wraps, however much she might wish it.'

'Perhaps she feels your father needs rest and quiet when he comes down here, and wants to discourage visitors,' Chessie suggested.

'You're joking, of course.' His tone was derisive. 'She regards his condition as a temporary inconvenience. I gather she's even planning to revive the Midsummer Party. Mark her return in style.'

'But surely...' Chessie stopped herself right there. If Linnet couldn't see that was inappropriate, it was no concern of hers.

'It's so good to be back here,' Alastair said softly. 'Know that there's someone on my side again.'

She thought, But I'm in no position to take sides—even if I wanted to—which is by no means certain.

She felt guiltily relieved when she heard Jenny coming noisily along the passage with the fresh coffee. The whole evening had been too intense—too bewildering, she thought. She needed time and space to think. To come to terms with everything that had happened. Not least with Alastair's sudden reappearance.

She should have been giddy with delight and relief. Jenny had clearly thought she'd find them wrapped round each other. Instead, she simply felt—stunned.

I have to adjust, that's all, she told herself defensively.

And her talk with Jenny would have to be postponed, too, which maybe wasn't such a bad thing. It would give her time to prepare, to work out a reasoned argument, instead of steaming in with all guns blazing, which had rarely succeeded in the past. She would have to be understanding, she thought glumly. Speak to Jenny woman to woman.

But what will I do if she won't listen? she asked herself unhappily as she drank more coffee she didn't want and her sister chattered away to Alastair.

'And I've got this wicked CD in my room,' Jenny was saying. 'I'll get it, so we can listen to it while we're finishing off the wine.'

'I don't think so,' Chessie intervened, feeling like someone's Victorian granny. 'It's getting late, and Alastair has to go. You have school tomorrow, and I must work.'

Jenny's scowl was immediate. 'Oh, for God's sake, Chess, don't be so wet,' she exclaimed impatiently. 'Tell The Ogre that his beastly meal gave you food poisoning, and you're having the day off. Don't you realise? Alastair's *back*.'

'Nice try, honey.' He grinned at her. 'But Chessie's quite right. Tomorrow's a working day for all of us. And there'll be plenty of other evenings—now that I'm back.' And he allowed his hand to rest briefly but significantly on Chessie's.

'You haven't a clue how to deal with men,' Jenny accused when he'd gone. 'I was going to put the music on, and leave you alone with him.'

'Not very subtle.' Chessie piled crockery and glasses onto the tray. *And what made you suddenly such an expert on men?* she wanted to ask, but didn't.

'Well, who needs subtlety—especially when you haven't seen each other for yonks?' Jenny sniffed. 'You were just sitting there like a stuffed dummy. No wonder he pushed off to the States if this is how you used to treat him.'

Chessie sighed. 'Love, I don't want to argue at this time of night. We're both tired. But I need to deal with Alastair in my own way. And at the moment, I feel really confused.'

Now, she thought, would certainly not be a good time to introduce the topic of Miles' extraordinary proposal. And, as far as Jenny was concerned, there would probably never be an optimum moment.

Besides, when the time came, she could always make up some story about feeling in a rut to explain why they were moving. So there was no real need to mention it ever to her volatile sister.

Because she was turning Miles down, and the sooner the better. She knew that, and she was comfortable in her decision.

Which did not explain why she spent much of the remaining night tossing and turning in her bed. And it wasn't Alastair's easy charm and smiling brown eyes that were keeping her from sleep, but a man with a scarred face and premature winter in his gaze.

And that, she told herself firmly, was ridiculous.

CHAPTER FOUR

CHESSIE felt edgy and out of sorts as she made her way to the small room adjoining Miles' study that she used as an office.

She'd cleared her desk the previous afternoon, so she was surprised to find a substantial pile of new script awaiting her attention.

Apparently, she wasn't the only one to have had a restless night, she thought, biting her lip.

She sat down with a sigh, and switched on the computer. Jenny had been irrepressible at breakfast, Alastair's name never off her lips. She plainly saw him as the romantic knight on the white charger who was going to solve all their problems and carry Chessie off to eternal bliss as a bonus, and Chessie had longed to put her aching head in her hands, and beg her to stop.

'I'll be a bit late this evening,' Jenny said as she grabbed her school bag and headed for the door. 'Choir practice.'

But Chessie, newly suspicious and hating it, saw that her sister did not look at her directly, and her heart sank.

She couldn't put off the inevitable confrontation for much longer, she reflected unhappily.

The distant bang of the back door alerted her to the arrival of Mrs Chubb, the daily help. And no prizes for guessing what would be her prime topic of conversation, Chessie thought as she made her way to the kitchen.

'You'll have heard, then.' Mrs Chubb, resplendent in a flowered overall, had already switched on the kettle for her first cup of tea of the day. She tutted. 'Poor Sir Robert. Who'd have thought it? Mind you, I always said he should never have gone to a hot place like Spain,' she added ominously. 'You should leave the Tropics for those who've been bred there. They can stand it.'

Chessie, contemplating Spain's new geographic status, murmured something neutral as she began to assemble Miles' coffee tray.

'And that means we'll have her ladyship back, coming the high and mighty,' Mrs Chubb went on. '"Call me madam," was what she told us all in the village.' She snorted. 'And a right madam she's turned out to be. Sir Robert at death's door, and her wanting Chubb to mark out the tennis court.'

'Actually, Sir Robert is expected to make a good recovery,' Chessie said, trying not to relish Mrs Chubb's unflattering remarks about Linnet.

Mrs Chubb sniffed. 'Not with her nursing him, he won't. Suffer a relapse, I shouldn't wonder. Make her a rich widow, and suit her just fine.'

'Mrs Chubb—you really mustn't...'

'I,' Mrs Chubb said magnificently, 'speak as I find. Chubb loves those gardens at the Court, and he'd never leave, but I'm not going back there to clean, not even if she doubled my hours and my money—which she won't.'

She poured boiling water onto her tea bag, compressing it until the water turned black, then added a splash of milk, and two spoonfuls of sugar.

'Proper tea, that is,' she remarked with satisfaction. 'Not like that scented muck that Madam drinks. Used to fair turn my stomach, that did.' She sipped with deep appreciation and nodded. 'Now I must get on,' she added, as if Chessie had been deliberately detaining her. 'The master left a note asking me to do out the spare room, so he must be expecting visitors. And about time, too. This old place could do with cheering up.' And she departed purposefully, mug in hand.

'The old place is not alone in that,' Chessie muttered as she spooned the rich Colombian blend that Miles favoured into the percolator.

While she was waiting for it to brew, she collected the mail from the box by the front door. Dealing with it was a simple process. All junk mail in the bin, all invitations to speaking engagements declined, all business correspondence opened and date stamped, and any personal letters placed unopened on Miles' desk.

Normally she hardly spared these a second glance, but today she found herself noticing that one of them came in an expensive cream envelope, with unmistakably female handwriting. And recalling that a similar item had arrived the previous week…

Oh, for heaven's sake, she adjured herself irritably. Anyone would think I were genuinely engaged to the man. Whereas nothing has changed. There is no personal relationship, and absolutely no reason for me to be in the least curious. And certainly not jealous.

And she added the cream envelope to the neat pile on the tray.

When the coffee was ready, Chessie carried the tray to the study and tapped lightly on the door. But there was no sound at all, not even the clatter of typewriter keys, so, after waiting a puzzled moment, she opened the door and went in.

The room had changed a great deal from her father's time, and she had never ceased to be glad of that. When the house had gone on the market, most of its contents had already been sold, leaving only the bare essentials. Miles had brought his own furniture, and had had Silvertrees redecorated too.

That, Chessie recalled wryly, had been one of the early bones of contention with Jenny, who couldn't be mollified even by the total refurbishment of their own accommodation.

But she herself had felt it right that the new owner should cut as many links with the past as possible. Stamp his mark on his new home.

The room was much lighter and more workmanlike these

days. Different books stood on the shelves that lined the walls, and that also held his stereo system and CD collection. A massive leather Chesterfield occupied pride of place in front of the fireplace.

The big imposing desk had gone, and Miles worked instead at a very ordinary table set by the window. His chair, however, had been specially made for him, with extra support for his spine.

Normally, he was at work by now, busy at the small portable typewriter that had accompanied him to so many places in the world.

'I thought you'd have had the latest thing in laptops,' she'd said once in the early days.

His mouth twisted. 'And how do you recharge batteries, Miss Lloyd, when there is no electricity?' He ran his fingers over the sturdy frame of the portable in a curiously caressing movement. 'This once belonged to my father, and he gave it to me when I got my first job in journalism. And I'll go on using it until the last spare part and the last ribbon have vanished from the earth. It's been my lucky talisman.'

'Not always lucky,' she said slowly, thinking of the mined road.

He shrugged, the blue eyes cool and meditative. 'We both survived, didn't we?'

But this morning, the chair was empty, and the typewriter hidden under its cover. Chessie set the tray down on the table, feeling bewildered. She organised Miles' appointments diary, and there was nothing that would have taken him away from the house at this hour.

Perhaps he was ill, she thought apprehensively, remembering Jenny's comment about food poisoning. But, if so, surely he'd have asked her to send for a doctor.

The room was very still, bathed in early summer sun, but the quality of its stillness told Chessie suddenly that she wasn't alone.

She trod quietly across the room and looked over the

high back of the Chesterfield. Miles was stretched out on its cushions, eyes closed, and his breathing soft and regular.

Well, Chessie thought, astonished. Another first.

She tiptoed round the sofa, and stood watching him for a moment. He was wearing the same clothes that he'd worn the previous night, indicating that he hadn't been to bed at all.

He looked much younger asleep, she realised with an odd pang, and almost vulnerable. The harsh dynamism of his features was softened and relaxed, the hard mouth gentler. The scarred side of his face was hidden, and his dark lashes, longer than she'd ever noticed, curled on his tanned cheek.

Chessie stood there feeling confused, and almost helpless. This situation had never cropped up before. So, what did she do now? Wake him, or leave him to the rest he obviously needed?

'Well, make your mind up, Francesca. The suspense is killing me.'

The softly drawled words nearly made her jump out of her skin, and she clamped her lips tightly on a yowl of surprise.

'You're awake.'

'I'm a light sleeper.' He sat up slowly, suppressing a grimace of discomfort. 'I learned a long time ago that it's better to know and be alert when someone's creeping up on you.'

'I was not creeping anywhere,' Chessie denied with dignity. 'I simply brought in your coffee and the post, as usual. And if you knew I was there, why did you let me go on standing about?' she added crossly, feeling a fool.

The sardonic smile flicked her. 'Perhaps I was hoping you'd wake me with a kiss.'

Chessie decided it was wiser to ignore that. 'Have you been up all night?' she asked, her brow furrowed.

He shrugged as he got to his feet, and stretched. 'It's something I do on occasion. I wasn't particularly tired last night, and I had a lot on my mind, so I went into the garden and sat for a while, then took a walk.' He paused. 'I gather you had a visitor.'

'Why—yes.' To her vexation, Chessie felt her face flood with colour. 'It's not against the rules, is it? And why were you spying on me?'

'I wasn't,' he said mildly. 'But like any householder, I'm interested in the identity of a stranger leaving my grounds after midnight.' He limped over to the table, and poured himself some coffee. 'I hope he didn't cause you any problems.'

'Problems,' Chessie echoed. 'Why should he?' *And what difference would one more make among so many, anyway?*

'I assumed,' he said, 'that he was Jenny's unsuitable boyfriend—the one you were so concerned about at dinner.'

'Oh,' she said. 'Oh, no. That was Alastair Markham—an old friend.'

'Markham?' Miles brows rose sharply. 'You mean he's connected to the spectacular lady we encountered last night?'

'Yes.' Chessie bit her lip. 'He's her stepson. His father's had a stroke, very sadly, so they've had to come back from Spain. And Alastair's come down from London to make Wenmore Court more—wheelchair-friendly.'

'And renew some old acquaintances.'

'Well, yes. Naturally.' Chessie lifted her chin. 'There's no harm in that, surely.'

'I think,' Miles said gently, 'that might depend on the acquaintance.'

'Are you claiming exclusive rights to my company on the basis of this—pseudo-engagement?' Her voice shook slightly.

'I'm not claiming anything at the moment.' Miles drained his cup, and replaced it on the tray. 'But when I do, you'll be in no doubt,' he added pleasantly.

He allowed her to assimilate that for a moment, then:

'How did your talk with Jenny go, by the way? Did you resolve anything?'

She could hardly tell him to mind his own business when she'd confided in him so readily twelve hours before.

'It wasn't a good time,' she said shortly. 'I'm going to take things up with her tonight.'

'Unless any more old friends drop by,' he murmured. 'You know, Francesca—'

His voice halted abruptly. Glancing across at him in surprise, Chessie saw that he'd picked up the cream envelope and was staring at it, his face suddenly taut.

'Is something the matter?' If he can spy, she thought, then I can ask questions.

It was a moment before he answered, and when he looked at her Chessie had the odd impression that he wasn't really seeing her. That he'd been away somewhere else, and his journey had not been a happy one.

'Not a thing,' he said coolly. 'Except that I need to shower, and get a shave and a change of clothes. And you, of course, have work to do.'

'Yes,' she said, and summoned a brief smile. 'Your walk in the garden must have been—stimulating.'

'It was,' he returned. 'Very. It happens like that, sometimes.'

She walked past him to the communicating door on the other side of the room that led into her office. She paused in the doorway, and looked back, just in time to see Miles slipping the cream envelope into the pocket of his trousers, his face cold and abstracted.

Clearly, it was something he needed to deal with in real privacy, she thought as she closed the door quietly, and sat down at the computer.

And, as she so badly needed to remember, it was no concern of hers.

Chessie found it irritatingly difficult to concentrate that morning. She faltered over the names of some of the

Eastern European characters in the story, although they should have been perfectly familiar to her by now. Also, the plot had reached a high point of drama and crisis, and some of the scenes were correspondingly tough and violent, which disturbed her as it had never done in the past.

I must be feeling ultra-sensitive today, she thought, crossly deleting another mistake.

She was almost glad when the last page was transcribed, saved to disk and printed off to join the mounting pile of manuscript in her out-tray.

She was dealing with the correspondence when Mrs Chubb popped her head round the door.

'Visitor,' she announced in a stage whisper.

'Oh.' Chessie got up from her chair. 'I forgot to ask him about that. Is the room ready?'

'Not that one.' Mrs Chubb flapped a dismissive hand. 'Madam's come calling. Strolled up the drive while I was doing the brasses, and asked for Mr Hunter. They're in the drawing room, and he wants you too.'

As she reached the drawing-room door, Chessie paused, smoothing back her hair with her fingers and taking a deep breath. Then, teeth gritted, she went in.

Miles, casually dressed in jeans and a white shirt, was standing by the empty fireplace, leaning against the mantel shelf.

Linnet, decorative in honey-coloured silk, was draped across one of the sofas that flanked the hearth.

'Such a bore, but no one was prepared to help at all,' she was saying, gesturing helplessly with one crimson-tipped hand. 'In the end I had to call one of the London nursing agencies, and they have someone who can start almost at once, thank heaven.'

'It must be a weight off your mind,' Miles agreed gravely. He looked across at Chessie, his expression giving nothing away. 'Hello, darling. I hope we can offer Lady Markham some lunch.'

'As long as it's not too inconvenient,' Linnet fluttered.

'I'm sure I must be disrupting your latest *oeuvre*.' She turned to survey Chessie, absorbing her simple blue chambray shift dress. 'In housekeeper mode today, sweetie?'

'That's what I'm paid for,' Chessie said lightly. 'Would soup and omelettes do?'

'I'd really prefer eggs Benedict,' Linnet said sunnily. 'But whatever you can manage will be fine, Chessie, dear.'

'Great,' Chessie returned with equal cheerfulness. 'Omelettes it is, then.'

The contents of the freezer in the storeroom adjoining the big kitchen were looking depleted. It looked to Chessie, hunting out the last carton of her home-made vegetable soup, as if she had a weekend of intensive cooking ahead of her.

She put the soup on the stove to heat through gently, set a bottle of Chablis to chill, then dashed to the dining room with the bleached linen place mats and napkins, and a handful of cutlery.

Back in the kitchen, she diced ham, grated cheese and chopped peppers, onions, tomatoes and salad potatoes to spice up the omelettes.

'Everything under control?' Miles appeared in the doorway behind her as she was whisking the eggs in a large bowl.

'The food certainly is,' she said crisply. 'I can't vouch for my temper.'

He leaned a shoulder against the doorframe. 'Then consider this your baptism of fire.'

'I prefer to remain unscorched.' She drew a steadying breath. 'I'm sure you'll excuse me if I don't join the lunch party. I'll have a sandwich in my office.'

'Then think again,' he said calmly. 'And lay a place for yourself in the dining room. I told you that I'd expect my future wife to help me entertain my guests.'

She said between her teeth, 'I am not your future wife.'

'Lady Markham thinks you are,' he said softly. 'Because you told her so, Francesca. And, as I've made clear, you'll behave accordingly until I decide otherwise. So it's lunch for three, and no arguments.'

She gave him a defiant glance. 'Is that an order—sir?'

He had the audacity to grin at her. 'Yes, ma'am.' He limped forward and perched on the edge of the table beside her. 'I'm seeing a totally new side to you, Chessie,' he remarked. 'All these months, you've behaved like a polite, efficient mouse. Yet now...'

'Overnight I've turned into a rat?' She glared at him.

Miles laughed. 'I was thinking of something altogether more feline—a tigress, maybe.'

Chessie looked down at the froth of eggs in her bowl. There was something about this turn in the conversation— a note in his voice perhaps—that disturbed her. That, and his proximity.

She said crisply, 'Now you're being absurd. And if you want me to feed your guest, I'd better get on.'

'Presently,' he said, and his voice was soft, the blue eyes narrowed in speculation. 'I've seen your claws, Chessie. But now I'm wondering if I might just make you purr.'

The egg whisk dropped from her hand, clattering to the tiled floor as he reached for her, pulling her into his arms with a stark purpose that defied resistance. She was held against him, trapped between the hard muscularity of his thighs. One arm lay across her back like a band of steel. His other hand shaped the slender curve of her hip as he smiled into her eyes.

Her lips parted to protest—perhaps even to plead—but the words were stifled by his mouth. At first it was a quest—a slow, controlled exploration. Firm but tender. Serious and teasing.

So many sensations—emotions—building inside her as he quietly and deliberately ravished her mouth. She hung in his arms, her limbs turning to water, tiny sparks of light dancing behind her closed eyelids. And her hands, braced against his chest in a vain attempt to push him away, crept upwards to fasten on his shoulders.

And everything changed. He pulled her closer still, kissing her deeply, hungrily, making no more concessions to her relative inexperience, or the fact that it was still the first intimate contact between them.

Ruthlessly, her lips were pressured apart so that he could plunder all the inner sweetness of her mouth. There was no gentleness in him now. No coolness either. Just a fierce need driving him beyond tenderness, beyond consideration.

The high dam of his reserve had been breached, and she was caught in the torrent. Drowning now in unguessed-at desires of her own, her aroused nipples blooming against the wall of his chest, her fingers biting frantically into his shoulders.

Gasping, tasting him, breathing him, drawing the male scent of him deep into her lungs as the world spun dizzily around her. The warmth of his skin blazed through her thin dress. She felt the sudden clamour of her pulses, the surge of the dark, heavy blood through her veins.

And then, as if a light had been switched off, it was over, and she was free. Taking a shaky step backwards, then another. Staring at him with ever-widening eyes. Lifting a mechanical hand to touch her swollen mouth. Hearing nothing but the raggedness of her own breathing. And his. In a silence that seemed to go on for ever.

When at last he spoke, his mocking drawl scored her senses like a sharp blade. 'Well—that was—instructive.'

Her breasts were aching against the cling of her dress, her nipples white-hot pinnacles of excitement. And he could see that. Would know…

She crossed her arms across her body, hiding the evidence of her self-betrayal from his cynical scrutiny.

'Why?' she whispered hoarsely. 'Why did you do that? How did you dare…?'

'Because we were both curious,' he said. 'And now we know.' His smile was suddenly mocking. 'Besides, our betrothal needed a little local colour, if only to prevent the worldly wise Lady Markham becoming suspicious.'

'What are you talking about?' There were tears not far away, constricting her throat, burning her eyes.

'Most newly engaged couples can't keep their hands off each other.' Miles' shrug was almost casual. 'Your transparent innocence was doing my street cred no good at all.' He gave her a measuring glance. 'At least you look now as if you know you're a woman.'

'And is that supposed to be your excuse—your rationale for—for *assaulting* me.' Her legs were weak, shaking under her. Her mouth was throbbing, and she was trembling wildly inside, ashamed of her own response. Of the destruction of her defences. And wanting to hit back.

His brows lifted over blue eyes turned suddenly cold. 'Is that how you see it? Just remember, my sweet hypocrite, that I was the one who called a halt. And if we didn't have a guest, and a cleaner roaming the house,' he added softly, 'I would not have stopped, and you wouldn't have wanted me to.'

He allowed her to digest that, then sent her a smile, swift and impersonal. 'Now, I'll leave you to get on with lunch.'

Alone, Chessie slumped against the kitchen table, her hands pressed to her hot cheeks. The temptation to sweep the entire preparations for the meal into the bin, then pack her bags and walk out was almost overwhelming. But she couldn't do that because she'd signed a contract, which required a minimum of a month's notice. And there seemed little doubt that Miles would enforce it, if necessary.

So, she had four weeks to endure before she could legitimately make her escape.

She groaned softly. Twenty-four hours ago, she'd been settled. Not ecstatically happy, perhaps, but resigned—even contented. Now her life was in chaos, and heading for meltdown.

And the worst of it was that Miles' final jibe had been no more than the truth, she thought unhappily. For the first time in her life, she had wanted everything that a man had to give—and more. And she would have offered her entire self in return.

If he had allowed it, she realised, wincing.

Well, she would never let him get so near her again. For her remaining time in his house, she would revert to being the calm, efficient employee. She would fill the freezer, run the house, and finish transcribing the new book. And she would ensure a smooth transition for her replacement.

She retrieved the egg whisk from the floor and washed it, wiping the small pool of beaten egg from the tiles. There was a smear on her dress, too, and she didn't have time to change, but what the hell? Her appearance was immaterial after all, she thought with a faint shrug. Although she would have to comb her dishevelled hair, and disguise the more obvious signs of Miles' kisses.

She made a salad from mixed leaves, heated a French stick in the oven, then poured the steaming soup into pottery bowls and carried them through to the dining room.

'This is actually quite good,' Linnet approved as she tasted it. 'I'd no idea you could cook, Chessie.'

'I had to learn,' Chessie returned. 'And fast.'

'Of course you did,' Linnet said in a tone of such gentle understanding that Chessie longed to slap her senseless. 'And to have to do all this cleaning as well, when you'd always had a housekeeper of your own in the past.' She tutted. 'You must be absolutely worn out.'

Chessie raised her eyebrows innocently, 'Oh, didn't you notice Mrs Chubb on your way in? She's the real treasure round here.'

'Well, I wouldn't describe her in those terms,' Linnet said with a touch of tartness. 'And I'd have got rid of her surly brute of a husband too, only Robert wouldn't allow it for some reason.'

'Probably because Mr Chubb is one of the top gardeners in the county, and his family has worked for the Markhams for generations,' Chessie commented pensively. 'You're really lucky to have him. More bread?'

But Linnet was not finished yet. 'All the same, it must have been hard on you, having to take a subservient position in your old home. Although everything seems to be working out for you now.

'What a pity your poor father couldn't say the same.' She sighed. 'It's all such a tragedy, although Robert predicted it years ago, of course. He was so shrewd about these things. But somehow one felt that your father might just get away with it. He seemed to have a gift for survival.'

She turned to Miles, leaving Chessie flushed but mute with fury. 'So, how do you come to be in Wenmore Abbas? Don't you find it the most frightful backwater?'

'No, I was looking for peace and quiet, and some space,' Miles responded with cool courtesy. 'Silvertrees seemed to fill the bill.'

'All this and a domestic goddess thrown in.' Linnet's smile was honeyed. 'I have to admit, alas, that if it weren't for poor Robert's mishap, I wouldn't have come back here ever. But the prospect of anything else seemed to agitate him so dreadfully, I gave way.' She gave a little trill of laughter. 'But at least we've returned to find a congenial neighbour for a change. And a famous writer too. So exciting.'

'Francesca would be the first to tell you that I lead a very dull life,' he drawled. 'Although, occasionally, it has its moments.'

Chessie, aware of the lightning glance of amusement that he'd thrown her, felt her hands curl into impotent fists in her lap.

She was thankful that Linnet seemed to be tired of her as a topic, and had turned instead to her husband's illness, her reaction to it, and her determination to see that he had the best of care.

She makes herself sound like an amalgam of Florence Nightingale and Mother Teresa, Chessie thought wearily as she removed the soup bowls and prepared to cook her omelette.

Linnet was fulsome in her praise for this too. 'I wish I'd known Chessie was available,' she sighed. 'Or I might have snaffled her from you. But I suppose it's too late now. Rather a drastic step,' she added. 'To propose marriage in order to keep your staff, but I can appreciate that you wouldn't want to lose her.'

Miles' smile was silky. 'Fortunately Chessie has other talents apart from the purely domestic,' he said softly.

'I'm sure she has.' Linnet leaned confidentially towards him. 'I hope I'm not telling tales out of school, but Chessie was involved with my stepson years ago. She was little more than a child, of course, but *so* precocious.' She paused. 'You haven't met Alastair yet, of course.'

'No,' Miles said meditatively. 'But, apparently, I caught a glimpse of him last night.'

Linnet's fork clattered onto her plate. She picked up her napkin and dabbed at her lips. 'Really? I don't see...'

'He was paying a visit on Chessie and her sister,' Miles went on. 'I happened to be around when he was leaving.'

Linnet's smile was rather pinched. 'Well, he hasn't wasted much time.' She put her hand on Miles' arm. 'I'd tie Chessie down without delay. From what I remember, she used to be very smitten with him. When do you plan to announce your engagement?'

'We don't.' The words were out before Chessie could stop them. She saw Linnet's arched brows lift, and groaned inwardly.

'What Chessie means is that we prefer to keep the whole thing private,' Miles said smoothly. 'Inform only the people we want to know about it.'

'But you are going to buy her a ring. Call me old-fashioned, but I do think it's a convention that should be observed.'

Linnet's own 'convention' was a diamond cluster reaching to her knuckle. Chessie had always been surprised she didn't list to port under its weight.

'I couldn't agree more,' Miles said affably. 'I'd planned

to take Chessie into town this afternoon and rectify the omission. I've asked Atterbournes to have a selection of rings for us to look at, darling,' he added.

Chessie didn't trust herself to look at him. She said stiffly, 'I'd hoped there wouldn't be a lot of fuss.'

'I'll buy the smallest stone available,' he promised instantly.

Linnet made a fuss about pushing back her chair. 'Then I must leave you in peace to go shopping,' she exclaimed. 'No dessert, thank you, Chessie, dear, although fresh fruit is always so tempting. And goodbye for now, Miles.' She took his hand and clasped it. 'Although I'm sure we'll meet again very soon.'

'I think it more than probable,' he agreed impassively.

'I'll see you out,' Chessie said, trying not to sound too eager.

As they reached the front door Linnet turned on her. 'Take my advice,' she said brusquely. 'Get what you can out of him while it's on offer. Because it won't last. He's come down here to put the Sandie Wells thing behind him, but you're only a stopgap. Very soon he's going to realise that a few scars and a walking stick haven't reduced his pulling power by any noticeable amount, and he'll be looking elsewhere.'

Chessie lifted her chin. 'I bow to your expert knowledge,' she said scornfully. 'Goodbye, Linnet.'

She closed the door and leaned against it, struggling to control her temper, and the odd wave of misery that had attacked her suddenly from nowhere.

Linnet was a Class A bitch, and always had been, and she was stupid to let her remarks get to her.

None of this is real, so why should I care what she thinks? she thought. And wished she could find an answer to that that made any sense at all.

CHAPTER FIVE

CHESSIE marched back to the dining room, expecting confrontation, but was disconcerted to find it deserted.

So, I may as well revert to housekeeper mode, she thought, tight-lipped, as she began to clear the table. She carried the dirty crockery into the kitchen and started to load the dishwasher.

She still felt dazed at the way events seemed to have snowballed in the last twenty-four hours, but about one thing she was very clear. She was going to leave Silvertrees at the earliest opportunity. She no longer had any choice in the matter. Or reason to delay her decision.

As she worked she kept glancing over her shoulder, expecting to see Miles appear in the doorway at any moment. And what would she do when—if it happened? How would she react? That was what she found impossible to figure out. And that was why she knew she had to go.

She switched on the dishwasher, and stood for a moment, staring out of the kitchen window at the view she'd known all her life. It would be a wrench to leave it, but she had no choice. Things were spiralling out of control, and she was frightened—scared stiff of how Miles could make her feel, and what he might make her do.

What was the name Linnet had mentioned? Sandie— Sandie Wells? It sounded familiar, but she didn't know why. How strange, she thought, that she should have worked for Miles all this time, yet had only recently learned he'd once been in a serious relationship, and the name of the girl he'd loved.

Sighing, she walked out of the kitchen and back to her office. She sat down at her desk, drafted her resignation, and printed it. She folded the sheet of paper and put it in an envelope. She would leave it on Miles' table for him to find when he returned. He might have gone for a walk, as he sometimes did after lunch, or disappeared down to the cellar, which he'd had fitted out as a gym, for a workout. Or he might simply have decided to go up to his room for a rest.

She had not, however, expected to find him in the study, also gazing out of the window.

'Oh.' She checked in surprise. 'I didn't realise...'

'Is there a problem?'

'No—not really. I...' She looked down at the envelope she was clutching. Simply handing it to him in person had not been part of the plan at all.

'Is that for me?' He held out his hand. 'What is it?'

'Four weeks' notice,' she said, and swallowed. 'As specified in the terms of my contract.'

He opened the envelope and read the contents, his face expressionless. 'May I ask why?'

'Oh.' Chessie shrugged awkwardly. 'So many reasons.'

'I hope what happened between us earlier isn't one of them.' He spoke gravely.

'No.' Then: 'Well, yes—a little, perhaps.'

'You've been kissed before.' His tone was dry.

'Of course.' *But not like that. Never like that.* 'All the same, it was something that shouldn't have happened.'

'If you're waiting for me to apologise, or even express a word of regret, then you'll wait a long time,' he said. He paused. 'You have another job to go to?' He spoke with courteous interest—no more.

'Not yet.' Chessie kept her own voice steady. 'But I will.'

'Naturally.' His mouth twisted. 'You're an excellent worker.'

Was that really all he had to say? she asked herself in bewilderment.

She said, 'Do you want me to draw up an ad for my replacement?'

'I think I'll use an agency instead.' He was silent for a moment, looking down at the paper in his hand. Then his eyes met hers. He was smiling faintly. 'Is this an oblique way of telling me you won't marry me?'

Chessie bit her lip. 'That was never going to happen. You must have known.'

He shrugged. 'It seemed to make a lot of sense. I hoped you'd think so too.'

'I'm sorry.' She shook her head. 'But I don't see marriage as an expedient.'

'Ah,' he said softly. 'Love or nothing. Is that it, Francesca?'

'You don't think that's possible?'

'I think it might well depend on where you went looking for love.' He spoke crisply, glancing at his watch.

Clearly, the interview was at an end. Her resignation accepted and confined to history, thought Chessie, feeling oddly deflated.

She lifted her chin. 'I'm sorry. Am I keeping you from something?'

'Our appointment at Atterbournes is in an hour's time.' He sounded matter of fact. 'I thought you might have things you want to do first.'

'Atterbournes,' Chessie echoed, staring at him. 'But I don't understand.'

'We're going to buy an engagement ring. I mentioned it at lunch.'

'Yes.' Her head was spinning. 'But I didn't think you meant it.'

'I rarely say what I don't mean. I thought you'd have realised that by now.'

She said wildly, 'But I'm leaving. You know that— you've agreed. Under the circumstances, you can't mean us to go on with this ridiculous pretence.'

'Oh, but I do,' Miles said gently. 'And when the four

weeks are up, we can stage a spectacular quarrel, or simply cite irreconcilable differences and part in a civilised manner. The choice is yours.'

She gave him an inimical look. 'I choose to stop now.'

He shrugged. 'Not on offer, darling. Besides, you'll be job-hunting soon, and you're going to need a reference,' he added silkily. 'So, you'll work out your notice on my terms. And I require the current arrangement to continue.'

'That's blackmail.' Her voice shook.

Miles tutted reprovingly. 'Think of it as pragmatism. A simple and practical exchange of favours.'

If she'd only had herself to consider, she'd have wished him to hell and back, and walked out, but there was Jenny, who had important exams coming up. She couldn't afford to make them both homeless.

She bent her head. 'Very well.' Her voice was colourless.

'Cheer up, Francesca.' His tone was mocking. 'Only four weeks to endure. You'll take it in your efficient stride.'

Will I? she thought. *Will I?*

She said, 'But I won't wear a ring.'

'Not negotiable, I'm afraid,' Miles drawled. 'I think it's wise—with all these old friends around. But I'll make sure it's the smallest stone available, if that makes you feel better,' he added, his mouth twisting.

She said fiercely, 'I am not your property. You cannot—mark me.'

He threw back his head, and the blue eyes burned into hers. 'I could,' he said. 'And we both know it. Or do you require further proof?'

Chessie was the first to look away. 'No.' Her voice was barely audible.

'Another sensible decision. You see how easy it all becomes?'

All I see, Chessie thought as she went back to the flat to change, is that I could be heading for the four most difficult weeks of my life.

*   *   *

Atterbournes was an old-fashioned family jewellers, occupying double-fronted premises in the High Street. There
was a thick Turkey carpet on the floor, and several highly
polished tables, with comfortable chairs, set at discreet distances from each other, where negotiations could take place
in appropriately hushed tones.

Chessie's first pair of earrings had been bought there,
and the string of real pearls her father had given her for
her eighteenth birthday, she remembered with nostalgia as
she lingered for a moment, scanning one of the window
displays.

I wonder what happened to it all, she thought regretfully
as the shop bell tinkled their arrival.

She felt absurdly self-conscious as the current Mr
Atterbourne advanced, smiling, to welcome them and lead
them to a table where a velvet cloth had already been
spread.

'Miss Lloyd, how very good to see you again, and on
such a joyous occasion.'

She murmured, 'Thank you', and sat down, aware of the
ironic look Miles had flicked at her.

A flat leather case was brought and ceremoniously
opened, and Chessie almost blinked at the coruscating array
of stones thus revealed.

My God, she thought. Even the least of them must be
worth several thousand pounds. Is Miles completely crazy?

'Now this,' Mr Atterbourne was saying, 'is a particularly
fine solitaire.'

She was all set to protest, then remembered just in time
that she'd agreed to go on with this farce. So, she held out
her hand in mute resignation, and allowed the ring to be
slipped onto her finger.

One by one, she tried them on, solitaires, marquises,
three- and five-stone bands and clusters, listening to Mr
Atterbourne murmuring about carats, and colour, and the
various cuts that had been used. And she could see that
they were beautiful, but they did nothing for her particu-

larly. She felt it was like gazing into an ocean of frozen tears.

'Not seen anything you like yet, darling?' Miles prompted. 'What about this one?' He was holding out a cluster of diamonds, so large and magnificent that it made Linnet's ring look puny.

She looked at him indignantly, scathing words forming on her lips, and realised that although his face was solemn, the blue eyes were dancing with unholy amusement, and challenge.

It was not funny, and she knew it. There was no aspect of her current situation that was even remotely laughable, but she could feel her mouth twitching in response, and an uninhibited giggle welling up irrepressibly inside her. And Miles joined in, his shoulders shaking.

Mr Atterbourne looked surprised, then indulgent. 'Perhaps Miss Lloyd would prefer coloured stones,' he suggested. 'I have some good sapphires, and an especially beautiful ruby.'

Chessie pulled herself together. How could he have done that? she asked herself in total bewilderment. After all he's putting me through, how on earth can he make me laugh like that? And could find no answer.

'It's just so—difficult,' she said, and meant it. She sent Miles an appealing glance. 'Do we have to decide today— darling?'

'Yes, my love,' Miles returned softly, a warning note in his voice that only she could hear. 'We do.'

'Or we could make up a ring, perhaps, if Miss Lloyd has a preferred stone...' Mr Atterbourne was trying hard.

'Yes,' she said slowly. 'Actually I do have a favourite.' She paused. 'There was a ring I saw in the window just now. A square aquamarine, with diamonds on each side of it. Could I try that?'

Miles' eyebrows lifted. 'Aquamarines?' he queried. 'Aren't they semi-precious stones?'

'At one time they were considered so,' said Mr

Atterbourne, rising to his feet. 'But they are becoming increasingly rare, and consequently more valuable. The ring in question is part of our antique collection, and very lovely.' He beamed at them both, and hurried off.

The ring slid over her knuckle, and settled on her slender finger as if it had been born there. The aquamarine looked cool and pure in contrast to the fire of the diamonds that flanked it. Two pairs of them, set one above the other, she saw, as if they were guarding the central stone.

'The colour is deeper than many of its modern counterparts,' Mr Atterbourne told them almost reverently. 'It's a very good piece.'

Miles studied it, frowning slightly. 'Surely it's more a dress ring?'

'It's an unconventional choice for an engagement, perhaps,' the jeweller admitted cautiously.

'You wanted me to decide,' Chessie said steadily. Her gaze locked with Miles in challenge. 'If I have to wear it, this is my choice, and no other.'

He looked back at her, his mouth twisting in wry acknowledgement. He said, 'Then we'll take it.'

She watched it placed in a satin-lined box, and then in one of Atterbournes' distinctive suede bags. Mr Atterbourne clearly expected it to be presented to her later in some romantic ceremonial, she thought ruefully, accompanied by flowers, candles and champagne.

Whereas the only likely accompaniment was going to be one hell of a scene from Jenny, who couldn't be kept in the dark any longer.

She stifled a sigh, sneaking a sideways glance at her companion. His face was harsh, and set, his mouth a hard line. She found herself wondering if he was realising he'd just made a very expensive mistake, and was searching for a way to call the whole thing off.

Please, she wanted to say. We don't have to do this. I can tell people that I played a joke on you, and it backfired. And that I'm getting another job because I'm embarrassed.

But inside the car, he took the ring from its package, and turned to her. 'Give me your hand.'

Now—*now* was the time to speak. To offer him a way out.

Yet no words would come. Instead, she found she was obeying reluctantly, trying not to shiver as his fingers touched hers. As the gold band slid over her skin. She looked down at the clear blue sheen of the stone. Touched it, as if it were some kind of talisman that would keep her safe. Four weeks, she thought. Only four weeks.

'So,' he said. 'Why this ring?'

She shrugged. 'It caught my eye. And aquamarines are my birthstone, so I've always loved them. I had a pendant once…' She stopped abruptly, aware that she was giving too much away. 'Also, it's very beautiful,' she went on swiftly. 'And it's been worn by other women, so it has a history.' She didn't look at him. 'Besides, antique jewellery holds its value. You shouldn't lose out too badly when you come to re-sell it.'

'You're all consideration.' His tone was sardonic. 'But actually I'd prefer you to keep it.'

'But I couldn't possibly,' Chessie began, remembering with dismay how much it had cost.

'Look on it as a souvenir,' he said. 'Or even a reward for suffering, bravely borne.' He paused. 'Are you going to tell me what happened to your pendant?'

Nothing could have been further from her mind, yet, somehow, her lips were already shaping a reply.

'It was sold,' she said. 'They took everything. Left us with the bare essentials.' She hunched a shoulder. 'You saw how the house was.'

'I did.' He spoke gravely. 'And I'm sorry. That was a bad time for you.'

'Yes,' she said. She smoothed the aquamarine again with a gentle finger. 'But, strangely, it wasn't the jewellery that hurt most, or even the furniture.'

'What, then?'

'They took my old rocking-horse from the attic.' Her voice was bleak. 'I saw them carrying it out, and I wanted to shout at them to bring it back. Because one day my own children were going to ride it, and I needed it.' Her laugh cracked in the middle. 'I couldn't believe they'd actually take toys. Things that we'd loved so much. That had no value for anyone else.'

He said quietly, 'It's not a merciful process.' And started the car.

I've never told anyone that before, she thought, startled. Not even Jenny. Haven't let myself think about it. So, why now?

But she didn't want to go down that road, she told herself with determination. She couldn't afford to. Besides, she had more pressing problems to consider.

They were almost back at the house when he observed, 'You've been very quiet.' He paused. 'I hope I haven't resurrected too many sad memories.'

She said ruefully, 'I was more concerned about the immediate future, and how to tell Jenny.' She shook her head. 'Or even what to tell her. She's not exactly the soul of discretion.'

'Then tell her anything,' he said. 'Except the truth.'

She stiffened. 'I don't make a habit of lying to her.'

'What a pity she doesn't treat you with equal candour.'

There was no answer to that, so she sent him a fulminating glance instead.

'Tell her that you've accepted me on purely economic grounds,' he went on. 'Then later you can admit that you can't bear to go through with it, and you're pulling out completely. She'll believe you. After all,' he added, almost casually, 'why should any woman agree to marry an ogre?'

'Oh, God.' Chessie bent her head as the car drew up in front of the house. 'You know about—that.' Her face was burning, and she couldn't look at him.

'I certainly knew she had a rock-bottom opinion of me.'

Miles shrugged slightly. 'But the nickname was news to me, until recently.'

He must, she thought wretchedly, have overheard them talking at some point. How many times had she begged Jenny to control her wayward tongue?

'I'm sorry. I—I don't know what to say.' She paused. 'She's very young in some ways, and she hates what's happened to us so much. And I think you've become a symbol of that.' She swallowed. 'Although that's no excuse.'

'Don't worry about it.' His mouth twisted. 'She'll have even more reason to slag me off when she hears I'm going to be her brother-in-law.'

Please let me wake up, Chessie pleaded silently as she undid her seat belt. Let me wake up and find this has all been some terrible dream.

'And just to add to your list of worries,' Miles added as she got out of the car, 'my sister is coming for the weekend.'

'Mrs Chubb mentioned there was to be a guest.' Chessie bit her lip. 'Is she bringing her family too?'

'Not this time. Robert is taking the children to stay with his parents. So we'll have Steffie's undivided attention.'

Chessie stared at him, appalled. 'What on earth is she going to think?'

'She'll think I proposed to you, and was accepted. That was Plan A, if you remember.' He gave her a brief, ironic smile. 'She's looking forward to meeting you,' he added, and drove off.

Chessie made her despondent way indoors, and went to her office. There were two calls on his answering machine. One was from his agent, but on the second, the caller had rung off without leaving a message.

I really hate that, Chessie thought. If it's a wrong number, why can't they have the decency to apologise? She wrote Vinnie Baxter's request for Miles to call her back on the memo pad on his desk, then took herself off to the flat.

As she entered she heard a chair being pushed back, and Jenny appeared in the kitchen doorway, white with temper.

'It's not true. Tell me she's lying, and it's not true.'

Chessie's heart sank. So much for breaking the news gently, she thought, sighing inwardly. She temporised. 'You're early. I thought you had choir practice.'

'What?' Jenny stared at her in bewilderment, then flushed. 'Oh—it was cancelled. And don't change the subject, Chess,' she added heatedly. 'What's going on?'

'Just calm down, please.' Chessie lifted her chin. 'Who is supposed to be lying—and about what?'

'You—and that bastard you work for. I've been told you're going to marry him.'

'Who told you?'

'Lady Markham—Linnet. I was at the bus stop in Hurstleigh, and she stopped and gave me a lift. She said you were engaged to Miles Hunter. She talked as if I should know all about it. I told her she must be mistaken, but she just laughed.' Jenny's voice shook. 'Tell me she's got it all wrong.'

'No,' Chessie returned with an assumption of calm. 'I can't do that. I am engaged to Miles. We've just been in Hurstleigh ourselves, buying the ring. But I'd like to know what you were doing there,' she added coldly. 'Why didn't you come straight home from school, if choir practice was cancelled, as you're supposed to do?'

'My God, will you listen to yourself?' Jenny rolled her eyes to heaven, temporarily diverted. 'I'm not a small child. I can go into town, if I want.' She shook her head. 'I can't believe you, Chessie. How could you do this? It's obscene.'

'How dare you say that?' Chessie said furiously.

'Because it's the truth. How can you marry anyone when you're in love with Alastair? It's crazy—horrible. And especially when it's The Ogre.' She shuddered. 'Then it becomes revolting.'

'Stop that right now.' There was a note in Chessie's

voice that shocked them both. 'You will never talk like that about Miles again, understand? I won't allow it.'

'Chessie!'

'I mean it. Your attitude to him has been a disgrace from the start.' The words were tumbling over each other. 'He's kind and generous, and he wants to take care of us both, so, from now on, you start being civil at least.'

'But Alastair's back,' Jenny wailed. 'Why didn't you wait for him?'

'Because he didn't ask me to,' Chessie said steadily, steeling herself against the pang of remembered pain.

'But you can't be in love with Miles Hunter. You just can't.'

'I didn't say that.' Chessie dipped her toe into deep waters. 'But we have—an understanding, and our relationship will be based on that—not on some silly romantic dream.'

'I can't believe you've just said that.' Jenny sounded genuinely horrified. 'You must have let him brainwash you.'

'No,' Chessie returned. 'I'm just facing up to reality.'

'Then Linnet was right. She said you just wanted his money, and he was looking for a nurse. Oh, Chess, how can you?' She ended on a little wail of distress.

'Come and sit down.' Chessie led her firmly into the kitchen, and placed her at the table. 'Miles and I are engaged, but not for any of the reasons you think.' She took a deep breath. 'We're going to try and build a relationship together, that's all. See if we can make it work.'

'And if it doesn't?' Jenny's eyes were fixed on her painfully.

Chessie shrugged. 'Then we part friends,' she returned with an insouciance she was far from feeling.

'Friends,' Jenny said bitterly. 'When was he ever our friend? He'd never get anyone to work as hard as you do for the money, and he wants to tie you down so that you don't leave and make a life for yourself. You're just going to—*moulder* here with him. And he's an ice man. He has no feelings.'

For one burning, tingling moment, Chessie remembered the feel—the taste—of Miles' mouth on hers. The hunger in his lean body that had ignited her own crazy response. *No feelings?*

She swallowed. 'Well—we're not married yet. And I'm certainly old enough to make my own decisions. And while I'm doing so, you will behave,' she added sternly. 'So— no more of these secret pub crawls of yours.'

Jenny's flushed face wore an expression of mingled guilt and anger. 'I suppose *he* told you. He's always hanging round the garden at all hours being spooky.'

'Well, it's his garden,' Chessie reminded her levelly. 'And it wasn't Miles, anyway. Jim Fewston tipped me off.' She hesitated. 'He also told me you were seeing someone. Why didn't you tell me, Jen? You know I'm always glad to meet your friends.'

'For tea on Sunday, I suppose,' Jenny returned rudely. 'Do me a favour. Anyway, it's not a big thing, so don't fuss.'

'Has he at least got a name?'

'Zak,' Jenny conceded reluctantly. 'Zak Woods. He works in the garage on the bypass.'

'Oh.' Chessie tried to conceal her dismay. She'd assumed he would be a sixth former at the local boys' school. 'How did you meet him?' she asked carefully.

Jenny looked down at the table. 'It was at that disco,' she said. 'The one I went to with Linda.'

But that was weeks ago, Chessie realised with alarm. And Jenny presumably had been seeing this Zak secretly all this time.

She steeled herself. 'Jenny, darling,' she said gently. 'You're going to take your exams in a week or two, and so much depends on them. Please don't do anything silly— that could affect the rest of your life.'

Jenny got to her feet. 'I call that rich coming from you,

Chessie. Sort your own life out before you start handing out good advice, why don't you? Because from where I'm standing, you're a complete mess.'

And she flounced out of the room and slammed the door.

Well done me, Chessie thought, wincing. I made a really good job of that.

And she couldn't really argue with Jenny's parting shot either. She was in total chaos, lost in a kind of limbo, and uncertain what to do next.

The thought of how different it all might have been could never be far from her mind, of course. If only Alastair had returned a week—even a day earlier. If he'd never gone away in the first place, she thought sadly, and been there for her to turn to when her life collapsed around her.

Linnet was bound to have told him about her engagement by now. She seemed hell-bent on spreading the news far and wide, and would have particular malicious pleasure in telling Alastair, as the tensions between them had clearly not abated.

And this time Chessie would not be able to act as buffer between them.

But it was little use sitting here, tormenting herself with what might have been. She might be wearing Miles' ring, but that meant nothing. It was still a working day, and she was his employee.

As she came back into the main part of the house, she saw a battered leather travel bag by the front door. She gave it a frowning glance, then continued into Miles' study. He was there, over by his table. He'd changed, she noticed at once, into more formal clothing—dark trousers, and a jacket with a shirt and tie, and he was packing papers into his briefcase.

Chessie checked, staring at him. 'Are you going somewhere?'

'I called Vinnie back,' Miles returned, without pausing in his task. 'She wants to discuss my schedule once the current book is in. So, I said I'd go up to London for a couple of days.'

'A couple of days,' she repeated. 'You mean you're going to stay up there?'

His glance was faintly derisive. 'You catch on fast, darling.'

'But you never do that. Where will you stay?'

'At the flat. That's what it's there for, after all.'

The flat, she thought, swallowing, that he'd once shared with Sandie Wells. That must have its memories. So why had he chosen this particular moment to return to it?

'You said once you were going to sell it.'

'And then I changed my mind.' He shrugged, and fastened his briefcase. 'At times like this, it's convenient.'

'Isn't this rather a sudden decision—to simply take off like this?'

'I used to be famous for it.' His voice was dry. 'But Vinnie's call seemed—opportune. It occurred to me that you've been under a lot of pressure, and that maybe you could do with some time and space to think about things. So, I'm letting you do just that.'

She stood very still, watching from the other side of the room, while a small frantic voice in her head whispered, Don't go. Don't leave me—please. Or—take me with you.

For a moment, she thought she had spoken aloud, and shock tightened her chest. Along with denial.

She said huskily, 'Are—are you getting the train?'

'No, I'm taking the car this time.'

'But it's late, and you've had a long day. You'll be tired…'

His brows lifted ironically. 'Why, Chessie, we seem to have skipped a bit. You sound just like a wife.'

She bit her lip. 'I'm sorry,' she said stiffly. 'Of course it's none of my business.'

'And you look a little fraught,' he went on. 'Surely it can't simply be concern for my welfare.'

'I've just been talking to Jenny,' Chessie admitted. 'I'm afraid I didn't handle it very well.'

'I suppose she told you she wasn't a child any more.'

'Something like that,' she agreed ruefully.

'In which she's perfectly correct, of course.'

'What do you mean?'

He said with faint impatience, 'You have to let her go, Francesca. If she passes these examinations of hers, she'll be off to college, and you won't be able to go with her to coddle her, and give way to her every whim.'

'I don't…'

'No? Yet she has the best that money can buy, and you look as if you dress from a second-hand stall.'

She drew a quivering breath. 'How dare you?'

'I dare because it's the truth, however unpalatable.' His tone was dispassionate. 'You spend your time endlessly making up to Jenny for something that wasn't your fault in the first place. But it's time you pushed her out of the nest, and started taking care of yourself instead. Or else find someone who'll do it for you.

'But what you can't do is live her life, and make her choices for her. She has to be able to make her own mistakes, and you have to let her.'

She stiffened defensively. 'And what makes you such an expert?'

'Personal experience,' Miles said drily. 'I can remember stretching parental tolerance to the limits, and Steffie was even worse. Jenny isn't the first girl to find an unsuitable boyfriend. I presume he's one of the stumbling blocks.'

'She met him at a disco on St Patrick's Night, and she's kept quiet about him all this time. And it's not even one of her fellow students. He's a garage mechanic, called Zak.'

'So, he can afford to take her to places like The White Hart. That will be part of the attraction, of course. And the fact that you'd disapprove, as you've just demonstrated, which makes him forbidden fruit, and all the sweeter.' He shrugged. 'All perfectly normal, so far.'

She said, 'I thought Jenny and I had a different relationship.'

'She's striking out for herself,' he said. 'And giving you the opportunity to do the same.' He paused. 'How did she take our engagement?'

'Not well.'

His mouth twisted. 'Hardly a surprise either. But maybe my absence will help there, too. Give her a chance to accustom herself. Let you build a few bridges.'

She said, 'But your sister's coming to visit.'

'I haven't forgotten. In fact, I shall be bringing her back with me.'

She followed him into the hall, feeling oddly lost. 'Is there anything special you'd like me to cook?'

'I leave it to your good judgement. But don't work too hard. Take a break, and relax a little. Regard it as a bonus,' he added drily. He paused. 'You don't have to cook on Saturday night, by the way. Your friend Lady Markham rang just now, and asked us up to the Court.' He sent her a brief, taut smile. 'Something for you to look forward to.'

'Oh,' she said. And: 'Yes.'

'I should be back about mid-afternoon on Friday,' he went on. 'But I don't foresee any problems during my absence.'

Except, she thought bleakly, that I *really* don't want you to go. And that scares me.

She stood at the top of the steps, watching him drive away, then turned slowly and went back into the house.

Emptiness closed round her. And silence.

She thought, I'm just so used to him being here. He's become part of everything I do. And now he's gone.

And realised she wanted very badly to burst into tears.

CHAPTER SIX

CHESSIE sat on the bottom stair, arms wrapped tightly round her body as she struggled to regain control of her emotions. She was frightened and bewildered. Unable to make sense of her own reactions.

But the simple truth was that watching Miles drive off had been like a wound in the heart. Something she could neither understand nor explain.

When Alastair had left, she had cried into her pillow, but it had never occurred to her to swallow her pride and beg him to stay. Yet that was what she'd been tempted to do only minutes before.

I'd have pleaded with him, she thought, astonished, if it would have done any good.

He had kissed her until she'd melted in his arms, bought her a ring, and walked away from her, and she was at a loss to explain any of it. Especially her own sense of desolation now that he'd gone.

He'd offered her space, and now she was standing in the middle of a vast and echoing wilderness.

She got slowly to her feet. There was no point in sitting here brooding. He'd gone, and he would not be back until Friday.

Three nights, two whole days, and a morning before she saw him again.

The precision of her calculation made her shiver. I must, she thought, be going mad. Cracking up. Because *this is not me*.

I should be using this time—his absence—to prepare for my future. For the day when I walk through that door, and don't look back. Or come back.

Of course, Miles himself might not come back. Maybe he'd decided that he didn't want to deal with her problems, or go on with this charade, even on a temporary basis, and planned to stay away until the month was up.

He was not, she thought, someone who would be good at saying goodbye.

He'd told her not to work—to relax, and treat his absence as a holiday—but that was impossible. She felt as if she were strung up on wires.

Besides, there was always something to do when Miles was busy with a book. He was tough on himself, drafting and re-drafting, then doing a final hard edit on the transcript she produced for him. She would see what there was in the alterations folder, and have the new pages awaiting his return.

She wandered into the study, and stood looking round her for a moment, at this place that was so definitely his domain.

It had always been very much easier to insist to herself that he was just a stranger. A man for whom she happened to work. And that when she went into her flat each evening and closed the door, he somehow ceased to exist.

But she knew now she'd just been fooling herself. Because, working with him so closely each day, she'd become quite intimately acquainted with him.

She knew, for instance, what food he liked, and that he preferred the linen sheets on his bed to be changed every three days. She knew that he favoured mellow earth tones over pastels, and natural fibres over man-made.

She knew that when he was thinking, he liked to walk round the room. That when he was putting his thoughts down on paper, he liked to play music. And that his only real superstition was the little portable typewriter sitting forlornly on his table.

If he'd left his lucky charm behind, then he must be coming back.

'He wouldn't go without you,' she said under her breath,

touching the yellowing keys. And what was she doing talking to inanimate objects?

She'd learned also to gauge his moods, to judge if and when his work could be safely interrupted, and by whom. And to know when he was in pain. Which were the good days for him, and which the bad.

And the past twenty-four hours would probably not get any gold awards. He'd asked her to marry him, for God's sake, and all she'd done was turn his proposal against him in order to score points off Linnet.

And the fact that she now wished the words unsaid a hundred times over made no difference at all.

There were only about twenty pages in the alterations folder. They wouldn't keep her occupied for long, she thought with a sigh. And she needed to stay busy.

As she turned away she noticed some torn scraps of paper in his waste basket, which she might as well empty now rather than wait for Mrs Chubb in the morning.

As she picked up the metal bin, she realised its contents were the tiny fragments of the cream envelope that had arrived that morning. For a moment, she stood very still, remembering his reaction to it. The way he'd slipped it into his pocket. And her own conviction that it was from a woman.

Was this the reason for his sudden decision to go to London? Could it be?

Despising herself, she sifted through the pieces, making sure that it was only the envelope that he'd thrown away, then shamefacedly dropped the bits back in the bin.

She had never in her life done such a thing before. She'd always regarded herself as discreet and honourable. Not someone who snooped and pried.

And if the letter had been ripped up and thrown away too, would she have got down on her knees on the carpet and pieced it together to satisfy her curiosity? Had she really sunk so low?

And was she simply curious, or was there a more fundamental emotion driving her on? Was it—could it be possible that she was actually jealous?

A shiver ran through her. She thought, I don't know who I am any more.

She needed to feel better about herself, and quickly too. Maybe she'd make a start on building one of those bridges with Jenny that Miles had mentioned. See if she could capture their lost rapport.

She left the bin and what it contained beside his table, and took the folder through to her office, then went back to the flat.

Jenny was on the phone when she went in. 'No, that's fine,' she was saying eagerly. 'I'll cycle over. See you later.' She replaced the receiver and turned to face her sister, her expression defiant.

She said, 'That was Linda. She wants us to get together this evening, and do some revision, and for me to sleep over. I said it was all right.' She indicated the phone. 'But feel free to call her mother, and check that it's really happening.'

Chessie bit her lip. 'Does it have to be tonight? I thought we might go into Hurstleigh, and go to the pizza place. Rent a video for afterwards.'

Jenny shook her head. 'I'd better go to Linda's. She's offered to go over a couple of things with me, and, as you keep reminding me, the exams are almost here.'

Which indicated that Jenny had been missing classes in order to meet with Zak, Chessie thought wearily. But this was probably not the time to make an issue of it.

'Anyway,' Jenny went on with a toss of her head, 'I wouldn't want to separate you from your lover. You have a relationship to invent. I'll see you tomorrow night,' she added over her shoulder as she went off to her room to pack.

Feeling oddly deflated, Chessie trailed into the kitchen and put the kettle on. Getting back on terms with Jenny was going to be more difficult than she'd envisaged, she thought, spooning coffee granules into a mug. And it was just as well her engagement to Miles wasn't the genuine article, or her sister's inimical attitude could have caused real problems. In fact she might even have been forced at some point to choose between them.

Although that was no contest. Jenny, after all, was her own flesh and blood, and needed her. She would always take priority.

But did Jenny necessarily feel the same about her?

The sheer disloyalty of the thought brought her up with a gasp of shock. That was Miles' fault, she upbraided herself, with all that talk of Jenny making her own life—moving away and moving on.

But perhaps it was wrong to rely too heavily on her sister always being around. Because clearly that wasn't going to happen. And tonight was a case in point.

She thought, I'm going to be alone here for the first time.

She supposed it was a step in the right direction. After all, if Miles was right, she was going to have to get used to the concept of being on her own. Of having only herself to rely on.

An evening, besides, when she could do exactly what she wanted, she reminded herself. When there would be no arguments about television programmes, or how loud Jenny's music should be. Or even the appropriate bedtime for a school night. That was for Linda's mother to deal with.

And Chessie was off the hook.

But once Jenny had departed, with the usual shouted goodbye and slammed door, the silence seemed to close round her.

Be positive, she adjured herself. Keep busy.

She got supper out of the way first. She didn't feel particularly hungry, so she made toast, and heated a tin of beans. While she ate her unexciting meal, she cheered herself up, making notes about far more adventurous menus for the weekend ahead, and beyond.

Without the car, she wouldn't be able to get to the supermarket on the other side of Hurstleigh, but Miles preferred her to use the smaller local shops anyway, and had opened accounts at most of them. So, all she had to do was to hand in an order, and the meat, groceries and vegetables would be delivered to the house later the same day.

Which would leave her time to do a little shopping on her own account, she thought. Miles' acid comment about her wardrobe might have rankled, but she couldn't deny its justice. She rarely bought herself any new clothes, and when she did she was attracted by hard-wearing qualities rather than fashion.

But if she had to compete in the market-place for a new job with good pay and some prospects, she'd need to pay some attention to her appearance.

And that was the route she had to take, or she'd be in danger of making an abject fool of herself. She needed to distance herself from Miles Hunter as quickly and completely as possible. Today's events had convinced her of that. And she needed to cling to that conviction.

Supper over and cleared away, Chessie took a long and leisurely bath, revelling in the fact that there was no Jenny banging on the door demanding admittance. She washed and dried her hair, slathered moisturiser on her face, then, wrapped in her elderly towelling robe, gave herself a manicure, watching a thriller she'd missed at the cinema.

Missing it might have been a good move, she decided restively halfway through. Even though it was brilliantly acted, it was too dark and violent for her taste, and not the wisest choice to watch alone.

She switched it off, and, to cheer herself up, decided to paint her toenails as well with the soft coral polish she'd purloined from Jenny's dressing table.

But with that task completed—what?

She tried reading her library book, but the story failed to grip her attention. She turned on the radio, and station-hopped, in an unavailing attempt to find some music she liked.

Oh, this is ridiculous, she thought crossly. I have all this time to do whatever I like, yet there's nothing I want to do.

Perhaps she'd just have an early night. After she'd been round the house, and checked it was secure. Something that Miles normally did himself, of course. The ground floor doors and windows were all locked, but she decided to go upstairs and make sure Miles had closed his bedroom window before he left. He had a habit of forgetting it, as Mrs Chubb often pointed out.

And this time was no exception. The thick carpet was soft under her bare feet as she went to the window and fastened the latch. As she turned she glimpsed a movement and froze, only to realise she'd seen herself, like a pale ghost, in the wall mirror.

She gave a nervous giggle, and stayed where she was for a moment, waiting for her heart to stop racing.

It was a very masculine room, she thought. When her father had used it, there'd been ornaments—pictures on the wall. After her mother had died, he hadn't changed a thing.

But now, the room was as bleak as a monastic cell. No softening touches at all—rather like his writing, she decided rather sadly. Except, she supposed, for the wide bed with its dark green quilt. That was definitely an indulgence.

Obeying an impulse she barely understood, she walked across the room and stood beside it, remembering how he looked when he was asleep. Imagining his dark head on the pillow now.

She bent, smoothing the already immaculate pillowcase with her hand, and the faint, familiar scent of his cologne reached her. She stepped back abruptly, with a little gasp. Because, in that moment, she'd been aware of him so vividly, it was as if his hand had clasped hers and drawn her down into the bed beside him.

But that was nonsense, she told herself vehemently. For

Miles was a long way from here, in another bed, in a room she'd never seen. And perhaps not even alone…

The breath caught sharply in her throat. It was time she got back to where she belonged, and stopped letting her stupid imagination run away with her.

Whoever shared his bed, in London or here, it would not be her. And that was her decision. Her choice.

Except for this one night, when she was alone, and so lonely, so isolated in this big house that she wanted to moan with the pain of it. And where to sleep where he slept might bring a kind of comfort.

No one, she thought, will ever know.

She loosened the belt of her robe, and let it fall to the floor, then lifted the edge of the quilt, and slipped beneath it, burying her face in his pillow, and breathing the scent of him into her starved lungs.

The linen felt cool against her skin as she sank weightlessly into the mattress, and gradually the tension and the trembling seeped away, leaving a strange peace in its place.

She should not be here, and she knew it, yet there was nowhere she would rather be.

And as her eyes closed, and she began to drift away, Chessie heard herself whisper his name.

When she awoke, the sun was streaming in through the window. For a moment, she lay, stretching languidly, totally disorientated, wondering who had opened her curtains, then she remembered where she was, and sat up with a gasp of alarm.

One glance at the clock on the night table told her that it was late, and that she'd overslept.

'Oh, no,' she groaned, stumbling out of bed and grabbing up her robe. Supposing Jenny had decided to come back last night, and found her missing—or Mrs Chubb had arrived early. What possible explanation could she offer for her extraordinary behaviour?

She didn't even understand it herself, but, at the same

time, she couldn't deny she'd had her best night's sleep in months, she thought breathlessly as she straightened the bed, erasing any tell-tale signs of her occupancy.

Back at the flat, she showered quickly and dressed in a navy cotton skirt and white blouse. Before leaving her room, she took off the aquamarine ring and put it back in its box, hiding it in a drawer.

Mrs Chubb would spot it in an instant, she thought ruefully, and she couldn't face the kind of eager interrogation that would follow, or the nine days' wonder that the good woman would set off in the village.

By the time Mrs Chubb arrived, Chessie had made the coffee, and was able to greet her with a semblance of composure.

'Off to London, is he?' Mrs Chubb said comfortably. 'Well, a gentleman needs to enjoy himself from time to time.' She nodded. 'Perhaps I'll give that room of his a good turn out. Make it nice for him to come back to.'

She shook her head. 'Not like poor Sir Robert. Chubb says there's wheelchair ramps everywhere at the Court, now. They're bringing him back by ambulance tomorrow, and a trained nurse with him.' She sniffed. 'And all Madam can think of is the parties she's going to give.'

'I'm sure she's very concerned about him,' Chessie said without any real conviction. 'Besides, it will probably cheer Sir Robert up to have company in the house,' she added more positively. 'It would be awful if he thought people were avoiding him because he's ill.'

'Well,' Mrs Chubb said tolerantly, 'you were always one to think the best of people. You just be careful you're not taken in, that's all.' And she collected her polish and dusters, and departed with a portentous nod of the head.

Chessie picked up a plastic bin liner, and headed back to begin the arduous task of sorting out her clothes. She was determined to be ruthless. A symbolic clear-out, she told herself with determination. Off with the old life, and on with the new. And in future she would not be trying to turn herself into the invisible woman either, she added silently, ramming a handful of washed-out tee shirts into her sack.

There was a daunting amount of space in her wardrobe when she'd finished. She would have to dip into her carefully garnered savings, and maybe use the credit card she'd been keeping for emergencies only.

Well, so what? Chessie thought, shrugging mentally. I've tried to be cautious and sensible, and look where it's got me. I'm just a confused mess. But by this evening, at least I'll be a better-dressed confused mess.

It clouded over during the afternoon, and when Chessie emerged from the last boutique she found it had begun to rain a little.

She grimaced faintly as she looked up at the sky, wishing she'd remembered her umbrella. But a little drizzle wouldn't kill her, and there was a bus due in ten minutes.

She'd forgotten how enjoyable a few hours of pure self-indulgence could be, she thought as she made her way along High Street. She'd concentrated on work clothes, and her first and most expensive purchase had been a smart black jacket. She'd chosen a couple of skirts, one in black, the other in grey check, and a handful of contrasting tops. Finally, she'd added a pair of black medium-heeled pumps, and a matching leather bag.

In addition she'd treated herself to several pairs of casual cotton trousers, some cheap tee shirts in clear, cool colours, and even a couple of summer dresses. She'd also replenished her underwear drawer.

That was the plus side, she thought. On the minus side, the first jobs agency she'd visited had told her with polite regret that they could already fill any temporary posts with the staff already on their books, and the second hadn't held out any great hopes either.

The prices being charged for rental property in the area had made her whistle too.

But it was still early days, she told herself. And something would turn up eventually.

Her carrier bags were weighing heavy by the time she arrived at the stop, and joined the end of the queue. The rain was heavier now, and she was beginning to feel damp and chilly.

The bus was late too, she realised with exasperation, transferring her bags from one hand to the other.

A car going past on the other side of the road slowed, then stopped, and someone called out her name. She glanced across, and saw Alastair beckoning to her. With a sigh of relief, she heaved up her bags and started across the road, where he was waiting with the boot open.

'Thank you,' she gasped.

'It's lucky I saw you,' he returned. He looked at the names on the carriers, and his brows lifted. 'Shopping for your trousseau?'

The query had a bite to it, and Chessie flushed. 'No, I just needed some new clothes.'

Alastair switched on the engine, then sat, watching the rhythmic swish of the windscreen wipers, but making no attempt to move off.

'So you're going to marry Miles Hunter,' he remarked eventually. 'Well, that should solve a whole lot of problems for you.' He turned and looked at her reproachfully. 'Why didn't you say something the other night, Chess? Why did you let me ramble on like that?'

She said quietly, 'Because I hadn't told anyone, least of all Jenny.'

'Linnet knew.' His sense of grievance was strong in his tone.

She bit her lip. 'Well—that was a mistake. It just—slipped out.'

'It's an odd feeling,' he said slowly. 'To come back, and find your girl's engaged to someone else.'

'Your girl?' Chessie echoed. She shook her head. 'After all this time without a word? You can't be serious.'

'But I'm back now,' he argued. 'Surely that changes things? I know I should have kept in touch, but you can't have forgotten how happy we were together.'

She said slowly, 'That was a long time ago, Alastair. Things have changed. *We've* changed.'

There was a silence, then he said in a low voice, 'Why are you doing this, Chess? You can't love him, and it's odds on that he's not in love with you.'

She lifted her chin. 'How can you possibly know what we feel about each other?'

He said gently, 'Chessie, you're a lovely girl, but he was living with Sandie Wells, for heaven's sake. They were a huge item.'

'So I keep hearing.' She frowned. 'Am I supposed to know who she is?'

He sighed. 'You must have heard of her. She was a top model before she turned to acting. She was in that film about jewel thieves, and she's done loads of television, too. Amazingly beautiful girl,' he added. 'With legs up to her forehead.'

'I really don't remember,' Chessie said quietly. 'But I have had other things on my mind.'

'Well, she dumped your fiancé pretty brutally, I understand, but rumour says he's still hung up on her, even though she's been married to some electronics millionaire for the past year.'

'She's moved on,' Chessie countered. 'Perhaps Miles feels it's time he did, too.'

He grimaced. 'Come off it, sweetheart. If he thought there was a chance of getting her back, he wouldn't give you a second thought.'

She drew a swift, uneven breath. 'May we change the subject, please?'

He gave her a surprised look. 'Yes, of course. I just thought you should know the score, that's all.' He paused. 'After all, I wouldn't want you to get hurt. And you could.'

That was true, she thought. Because she was hurting already, a knife twisting slowly deep within her.

The car moved off, and Chessie sat silently, looking down at her hands clasped in her lap. If she'd been harbouring any illusions about Miles' reasons for proposing to her, they'd have been shattered for ever. Every time he looked at her, she thought painfully, he would be drawing comparisons between her and the amazing beauty he'd lost. And when he touched her…

Her mind closed off in rejection. She could never allow that to happen again, she told herself starkly. Never permit herself to forget everything in his arms, under the subtle torment of his mouth. From now on, that was the forbidden zone.

It wouldn't be easy. Miles was an experienced man who knew perfectly well what he was doing. And he'd set out, deliberately and cynically, to expose the depth of that blind, unthinking need that she hadn't realised existed until his lips took hers. A need that would not—*could not* ever be satisfied.

And I shall have to learn to live with that, she thought. Somehow.

'I'm running low on petrol. I'd better get some.' Alastair's voice broke abruptly across her unhappy reverie.

'Yes,' she returned mechanically. 'Of course.'

It was only when he'd filled his tank and gone off to pay that Chessie realised they were at the garage on the bypass. She wound down her window, allowing a rush of cool damp air to enter the car, and looked around her.

It was a busy place, selling new and used cars as well as offering repairs, and there were mechanics in dark blue overalls everywhere. But one in particular caught her attention—tall, and coarsely good-looking, with his dark hair caught back in a pony-tail. There was a dragon tattooed on his arm beneath the rolled-up sleeve, and he wore a silver earring, and a nose stud.

As if aware of her scrutiny, he glanced towards the car, his expression one of surly indifference.

Chessie's heart skipped a sudden, alarmed beat, as her premonition sharpened. She thought, Oh, no. Please, no. Not him. It can't be…

Only to hear a voice call 'Zak' and see him look back over his shoulder, mouthing some obscenity.

Her hand crept up and touched her throat, all her worst fears confirmed.

'Are you all right?' Alastair swung himself back into the driving seat. 'You're as white as a ghost. What's happened?'

'Nothing,' she said quickly. 'It was just a bit stuffy in the car, that's all.'

'Do you want the air-conditioning on?'

'No, it's fine.' Closing the window, she summoned a smile, trying to ignore the churning in her stomach. *Jenny*, she thought. *Oh, God, Jenny.* 'Anyway, we'll be home soon.'

'Come back to the Court, and have some tea,' he invited. 'Linnet's not there. She's gone up to London to bring my father down.'

'Oh, how is he?' Chessie was thankful to focus on something else.

'No different, I gather.' He shook his head. 'I can't imagine why he's so set on being at the Court, anyway. The medical facilities in Spain were first class. And keeping the place up is a hell of a drain on his finances.'

'But it's his home,' Chessie said. 'And your inheritance.'

'I'm not sure I relish being saddled with a great barn of a place like that.' His tone was moody as he pulled off the forecourt, and waited for a gap in the traffic. 'I plan to be based in London. Or I might even go back to America if there's a suitable opportunity.'

She was aware of the faintly challenging look he sent her, and suspected it was her cue to react with distress. Beg him to reconsider. And for a brief moment, she was tempted. This was Alastair, after all, on whom all her girl-hood hopes and longings had been centred. She'd cared for him once. Maybe she would again, once she'd rid herself of the distraction of Miles.

Alastair, after all, showed every sign of wanting to renew their relationship, and perhaps she was a fool to hold back when he could well be the substance in her life, and Miles only the shadow. Time alone would show—only she didn't have that much time...

She wondered why she hadn't confided in him when he'd asked—expressed her fears for Jenny, and the feelings of instinctive revulsion that Zak had inspired in her. After all, Alastair had known her sister since she was a child, and who better to advise her?

Because she had to do something. And it wasn't just Zak's appearance that made her uneasy. Tattoos were fashionable, and so was body piercing. And she could see that his raffish good looks might have an effect on an impressionable girl.

No, there was something about him—some element in his body language or his attitude that chilled her, and it was pointless telling herself that she was being over-imaginative, and that Zak was probably kind to animals and good to his mother.

Because kindness was not in him, and she knew it.

'Am I invited in?' Alastair asked when they reached Silvertrees. 'I'd like to congratulate the bridegroom.'

'He's rather busy, I'm afraid.' Which was an evasion, Chessie told herself, and not a downright lie. Again, she had no real idea why she'd concealed the fact that Miles was away. Except that instinct told her that he would not appreciate her entertaining Alastair during his absence.

'Besides, we'll see you on Saturday evening,' she went on. 'Your stepmother has asked us to dinner.'

'Has she?' His surprise was genuine. 'It's the first I've heard of it.'

'Unless, of course, you think visitors would be too much for your father.'

His grimace was painful. 'To be honest, I don't know whether it will register with him that strongly. He's in a bad way, Chessie. And now, just when I need you, you belong to someone else.'

She said drily, 'How times change. A week ago, I didn't seem necessary to anyone in particular. I'm not used to being so much in demand.'

He took her hand, his eyes moody and faintly brooding. 'Just remember this, my sweet. If you change your mind, I'll be waiting.' He pressed a light kiss to her palm. 'Now, go in, before he gets suspicious.'

She found she wanted to snatch her hand away, but she made herself wait for him reluctantly to relinquish it. Then, with a murmur of thanks for the lift, collected her shopping and went into the house.

She only wished Miles were there, suspicious or not.

He was the one she could tell about Jenny. He would understand.

She needed to hear his voice, she realised suddenly. Wanted him to reassure her that the repulsive Zak was simply part of Jenny's belated adolescent rebellion. Her first foray into the adult world, even if it was with the wrong companion.

She badly needed to hear that it was an infatuation that would end as swiftly as it had begun, with her sister older and wiser, but with no real harm done. And that it would all come right in the end.

And she could talk to him about it, she thought. She could call him at the flat, and tell him what had happened. Pour out her fears and forebodings, and be comforted.

Even if he told her she was being a fool, it would help in some strange way.

She went into the study, found the number and dialled. Of course, he might not be there, she thought as she heard the ringing tone. He might be at Vinnie's office in the

Haymarket, and, if so, she would leave a message asking him to call her back, preferably this evening.

She heard the receiver lifted, and was about to rush into speech when she heard a woman's voice say, 'Hello?'

She thought, I must have got the wrong number. She wanted to say something—to apologise and ring off, and be more careful next time. But she couldn't speak. Because her heart was beating frantically, and a hand seemed to be tightening round her throat.

'Hello?' the voice repeated, more forcefully. Then: 'Miles—there's no one there.'

And Chessie found herself letting the receiver drop back onto its rest as if it had suddenly become red hot and burned her fingers to the bone.

She realised she was kneeling on the floor, bent double, gasping for breath, her arms wrapped protectively round her body. While all the time a small, desperate voice in her head was whispering, What shall I do? Oh, God, what shall I do?

CHAPTER SEVEN

WELL, what had she really expected? Chessie asked herself wearily, peeling onions as if her life depended on it. Miles was a man, and, as she knew only too well, possessed of all the usual male instincts. And to be fair, he had never indicated that he was celibate.

And, anyway, it was none of her business, whatever she might have suspected.

It was something she'd repeated to herself at intervals during the course of the previous day, and two restless nights, until the words seemed to hammer at her brain.

But, she'd discovered, suspicion was one thing. Having it so openly confirmed was quite another, and she was still reeling under the impact. Still at a loss to know how to deal with the situation when he returned.

The letter in the cream envelope had, of course, been from the woman in his life, arranging an assignation. And one that he was keen to enjoy to the full, judging by the haste of his departure, she thought, biting her lip.

But if there is someone in his life, Chessie argued with herself, all over again, then why did he ask me to marry him? It makes no sense. Unless his unknown lady can't cook or use a computer, and he thinks I'm a better economic proposition.

She rinsed her hands, and wiped her streaming eyes on a piece of kitchen towel. At least she had an excuse for weeping this time, she thought wryly. She couldn't say the same for the tears she'd shed over the past twenty-four hours.

They'd been nothing but the purest self-indulgence, and she was disgusted with herself. Scared, too, because, in spite of all the traumas she'd gone through in the past, she'd never experienced such anguish in her life before.

Yet how could that be possible? And why was she beating herself up like this? After all, the rules of the game hadn't changed.

Because Miles' original offer had been a business proposition, and nothing more. He wanted her to go on running his house, and take on the additional role of his hostess.

And even if sex at some stage hadn't been entirely ruled out, it certainly hadn't been uppermost in his mind.

As indeed why should it be, when he had his London lady to fulfil his needs already?

He never at any time said he was in love with me, she reminded herself. And, anyway, I've turned down his proposal, and very soon I'll be out of his house, and his life altogether. So, it's ludicrous for me to behave as if there's been some kind of betrayal involved here. As if I have the right to be hurt by anything he does. Because Miles is a totally free agent, and so am I.

And I cannot—*cannot*—allow myself to care—even if he has a mistress for every day of the week.

Yet, knowing all this, how can it still matter so much—and so bitterly?

She heated oil in a pan, and began to fry chunks of steak. She'd been cooking all morning, concentrating almost grimly on the task in hand, whereas usually she found it a relaxation. She was now making a rich beef stew for dinner that night, to welcome his sister.

In a way, she was dreading meeting the unknown Steffie because it was inevitably going to mean more deception in the short term. On the other hand, her presence would curb any reckless bid by Chessie to venture into forbidden territory, and ask questions that were none of her concern. Which she had to admit would have been a danger otherwise.

She'd worked hard, trying to blank out the thoughts still reeling in her head. The house was full of flowers, the dining-room table was already gleaming with silver and crystal, and candles in tall holders waiting to be lit, and the scent of lavender and beeswax hung in the air thanks to Mrs Chubb's ministrations.

Chessie was determined that Miles would have nothing to complain of in the time before she left his employment. She would fulfil each and every one of her duties to the letter—including playing the part of his fiancée, if that was what he still wanted.

She would make sure she took glowing references to her next job.

Not that she was having much luck in that connection, she admitted, grimacing. She'd gone through the advertisements in the local paper, and rung the few secretarial posts on offer, only to be told they were already filled. She'd enquired after a position as a receptionist too, but the money was barely a quarter of what she was earning at the moment, and she'd hardly be able to keep herself in a bedsit, let alone contribute towards Jenny's student career.

It might be better to forget about working in an office altogether, she thought with a sigh, and find another residential post as a cook-housekeeper—only this time she'd ensure her employer was an elderly lady.

'Something smells good.' Mrs Chubb came bustling in. 'It'll be nice to have some company here for a change. I was saying to Chubb, it seems dead quiet here without Mr Hunter, even though he generally keeps himself to himself.'

But not always, thought Chessie with a pang, lifting the browned meat into a casserole dish.

She said, 'Mrs Chubb—do you know a Zak Woods?'

Mrs Chubb sniffed. 'Know of him,' she said. 'And not much good either,' she added ominously. She gave Chessie a curious look. 'Why do you ask?'

Chessie shrugged. 'Oh, someone mentioned his name.' She paused. 'He's a mechanic, isn't he?'

'So they say. Trouble-maker, more likely. Been one step

ahead of the law since he could walk. I wouldn't take any motor of mine near him.'

Who said things can only get better? Chessie wondered wearily when the good woman had departed.

She'd put her own problems aside the previous evening, and attempted, gently, to question Jenny a little. She hadn't mentioned that she'd seen Zak, and had tried to keep her questions friendly, concealing her instinctive anxieties about the relationship. But it had been no good. Jenny had made it angrily clear that she'd regarded Chessie as invading her privacy.

I'm out of my depth here, Chessie had thought tiredly as her sister had banged out of the room.

Now, as she poured wine into her casserole, it occurred to her that perhaps she'd been too protective of Jenny, and by doing so had driven her to break out, and seek an extreme like Zak.

What can she see in him? she wondered, then checked herself hastily, realising that she probably wouldn't like the answer, so it might be better not to know.

She could only suppose that Jenny had genuinely fallen in love with him, and love was said to be blind. Even so, surely she must sense the malevolence in him that Chessie had spotted in one brief moment? Or, in some ghastly way, was that part of his attraction?

She knew she had to tread carefully. Jenny was above the age of consent, and she could get married among other crazy things.

Maybe I've just got to be patient, and wait for this madness to run its course, she thought as she transferred her casserole to the oven.

And perhaps that's how I'll get over Miles too, she added bleakly.

She was waiting edgily at the open front door as Miles' car came round the curve of the drive and stopped on the gravel with a soft whisper of tyres.

Unobtrusively, Chessie blotted damp palms on her jean-clad hips, and composed her face into a smile.

Steffie Barnes was nearly as tall as her brother, and had the same blue eyes, but her hair was fairer, and she had a merry face and a warm, low-pitched voice.

'So you're Francesca,' she said, destroying Chessie's last frail hope that maybe she'd been the one answering the telephone in her brother's flat two days earlier. Her hand clasp was firm, and her gaze friendly. 'I began to wonder if I was ever going to meet you, or if you were just a figment of my dear brother's fertile imagination.' She turned, lifting a wry eyebrow in his direction.

'Oh, she exists.' Miles' drawl held amusement and something less easy to define. The blue eyes were cool and searching as they scanned her. 'Don't I get a welcome too, Chessie?'

Flushing, Chessie stepped forward, offering her cheek awkwardly. But Miles captured her chin, and turned her face to receive his kiss, swift and sensuous, on her lips. He did not release her at once.

'You've got shadows under your eyes.' He spoke softly, but he wore a faint frown. 'I hope they're because you've been missing me.'

'Why else?' Her smile was beginning to feel as if it had been glued there, but at last he let her go. She turned to Steffie. 'Would you like to see your room, and then have tea?'

'That would be fine,' Steffie accepted. 'Or I could always make myself scarce in the garden, and let you and Miles have a proper reunion.'

Miles laughed. 'We can wait. Give Steffie the guided tour, darling, while I check through the mail.'

As they went upstairs Steffie said abruptly, 'I owe you a vote of thanks. I was terrified that Miles was going to turn into a real recluse. Writing's a solitary occupation at the best of times, but he seemed to have no incentive to lead any kind of life outside working hours.' She gave a gleeful grin. 'Yet now here you are engaged to each other. And I couldn't be happier.'

Chessie flushed again. She said constrictedly, 'It's all happened so fast. I'm not really used to it yet.'

'I've been married for ten years,' Steffie said. 'And I still sometimes look at the face on the pillow next to me, and think, Who's that?' She gave a gasp of pure pleasure as Chessie opened a door onto late afternoon sunlight billowing off primrose walls. 'What a lovely room.'

'I've always loved it,' Chessie agreed quietly, putting Steffie's case on the bed.

Steffie gave her a quick glance. 'Was this your room—before? Miles filled me in on some of the background. I hope you don't mind.'

'Of course not.' Chessie made herself speak lightly. 'And—yes—this was mine.'

'Oh, dear,' Steffie said, then brightened. 'But it isn't as if I've turned you out or anything.'

'No. And the housekeeper's flat is really comfortable.'

'The flat?' Steffie was clearly surprised. 'You're not over there, surely?' She shrugged. 'I mean—you and Miles are going to be married. I assumed you'd be sharing more than a roof.'

'I live with my younger sister.' Chessie was suddenly floundering. Burning all over, too. 'It makes things—difficult.'

'I thought she was all grown-up with a love life of her own.' Steffie shrugged. 'But you know best. Or I hope you do.'

She opened her case and pulled out a dress, shaking out the creases. 'I appreciate this is something of a crash course in getting acquainted, but you don't have any reservations about Miles—his injuries?' She gave Chessie a straight glance. 'Because he's been down that road already, and it wasn't good.'

'Yes.' Chessie swallowed. 'He—he was very frank about it.' She glanced round the room. 'I hope you have everything you need.' She gestured awkwardly. 'I—I'll leave you to unpack while I go and talk to Miles.'

'You do that,' Steffie replied cheerfully. 'I'll make sure I sing loudly on my way downstairs.'

Chessie paused outside the study, bracing herself physically and mentally before she went in. Miles was standing by the window, looking out at the garden. He turned slightly as she came in, and smiled at her.

'It's good to be back.'

His smile wrenched at her heart until she could have cried out with the anguish of it. She stiffened slightly, defensively. 'I came to ask whether you wanted tea in the drawing room or the garden.'

'You decide,' he said. He paused, eyeing her meditatively. 'And for the duration of Steffie's visit, could you be primarily my future wife, rather than the paid employee?'

'I don't find it easy,' she said. 'Being a hypocrite.'

'Implying that I do?' The smile had gone. 'If you recall, I asked you to marry me, Chessie—not take part in a charade, which you set in motion.' He paused, allowing her to digest that. 'At least you're wearing your ring.'

She lifted her chin. 'I presumed you'd wish me to.'

'I hoped you'd want to,' he came back at her sharply, then sighed. 'Oh, God, Chessie, this is not what I'd planned. May we start again, please?'

'Perhaps we'd better.' She forced a smile. 'Your sister's very nice.'

'I think so too.' His mouth twisted. 'You must be relieved to find that I'm the only bastard in the family.'

He looked tired, she thought, his eyes shadowed, his facial muscles taut. But then there was an excellent reason for his weariness, and she felt her hands curl into fists at her sides as that swift, uncontrollable pain slashed at her again.

She found herself saying stiltedly, 'Did you enjoy your— time in London?' And waiting, scarcely breathing, for his answer.

'The meetings with Vinnie and the publishers went well.'
His tone was matter-of-fact. No guilty look, or sign of evasion. But then—why should there be? Miles had never offered her fidelity, she thought, sinking her teeth into her
lower lip. No promise had been broken.

No promise. The thought was an unwanted intruder, invading her mind. *Just my heart...*

'The next three years of my life are certainly spoken for,'
he added, while Chessie stood rigid, aghast at this moment
of self-revelation. Fighting for a semblance of composure.

She managed to say, over-brightly, 'Your new secretary
is going to be kept busy.'

'I'm sure she'll cope.' He was watching her again, his
eyes narrowed. He took a step towards her, and she fell
back a pace, the wary defiance in her eyes meeting the
incredulity in his.

For a few seconds the tension in the silence between
them made her nerve-endings jangle.

Then Miles limped across to the Chesterfield and sat
down. He said, quietly, 'I'd like you to come here, please,
and tell me what's wrong, because clearly there's something. You look like your own ghost.' The cool drawl
sharpened in warning. 'And don't put me to the trouble of
fetching you, Francesca.'

Chessie complied reluctantly, huddling into the opposite
corner, as far away from him as she could manage. She
could see from the tightening of his mouth that this wasn't
lost on him either, but she couldn't allow herself to worry
about it. She was battling for self-preservation here.

'Well?' The blue gaze was piercing.

She said, 'I've seen Jenny's boyfriend.'

'He came here?' His brows rose.

'Oh, no. He was at work—at the big garage on the bypass.'

He stared at her. 'Are you telling me you walked all that
way just to take a look at him?'

'No.' She hesitated. 'As it happens, Alastair was giving

me a lift back from Hurstleigh. I—I'd been shopping, and it came on to rain.'

'How good of him,' Miles said softly. 'But then he is an old friend.'

'He needed petrol,' she went on. 'And that's when I saw him—Zak Woods, I mean.'

'And?'

'Think of your worst nightmare,' Chessie said. 'Then double it.' She raised anguished eyes to his. 'According to Mrs Chubb he's lucky not to have a police record.' She shook her head. 'There's something horrible about him. I don't know how Jenny can bear it.'

'It might just be the attraction of opposites,' he said. 'Or it could be a punishment.'

'Who is she punishing?'

He shrugged. 'Herself, you, the whole world. Who knows?'

'She's going to ruin her life,' Chessie said wretchedly.

'I doubt that. The one good thing about nightmares is that you wake up from them eventually. Or so I've always believed,' he added drily. Then paused. 'So—what else is the matter?'

'I don't know what you mean.' Chessie shook her head, allowing a soft swathe of hair to fall across her suddenly flushed face. Her physical awareness of him—of his nearness—was acute. She was shaking inside, her mouth dry, an unfamiliar ache grinding deep within her.

'I think you do.' He was silent again, and she was aware of his gaze measuring her—lingering...

'I also think,' he went on, a wry twist to his mouth, 'that offering you a breathing space may not have been such a wise move, after all. I—really shouldn't have left you on your own.'

She drew a quick breath. 'That—that's nonsense. And I'd better go,' she added quickly. 'I have things to do— your sister's tea to get.'

Miles shook his head slowly. 'Steffie will wait, I promise. But I can't.'

She was starting to get to her feet as he reached for her. Caught off balance and vulnerable, Chessie found herself pulled backwards, his arms closing round her, so that she fell against him.

Gasping, she tried to struggle, but it was too late. Miles lifted her as if she were a featherweight, settling her, helpless and imprisoned, across his thighs.

'Much better,' he approved softly, smiling down into her outraged face as he lowered his mouth to hers.

She tried to fight him. To deny the hammer of her heart, and the quicksilver heat pulsing in her bloodstream. But she'd forgotten—or tried to forget—the deliberate beguilement of his lips, coaxing her mouth to open for him. And then—the warm, honeyed glide of his tongue against hers.

Her lashes swept down to her flushed cheeks. Her head fell back against his encircling arm as her body arched towards him, mutely, involuntarily.

'My love,' he whispered against her skin. 'My sweet love.'

He kissed her again, deepening his demand, compelling a reciprocation that she was powerless to deny, feeding the hunger he had incited with his first touch.

His lips pressed tiny kisses to her forehead, her cheeks, her eyelids, and the corners of her eager mouth. His hand soothed her throat, moving down to her shoulder, then down again to the first of the pearl buttons that fastened her white shirt.

He released them slowly, kissing her softly and sensuously as he did so, murmuring words of reassurance against her lips as if he recognised the swift, shocked hammer of her heart and sought to allay any last vestige of uncertainty.

The last button undone, Miles pushed the shirt off her shoulder, and looked down at her, his blue eyes slumbrous as they regarded the scraps of white lace that hid her breasts.

'Pretty,' he approved softly, then slid a questing finger under one narrow strap, slipping it down her arm.

'And exquisite,' he added huskily, brushing the loosened cup away from her rose-tipped breast, baring it for his caress.

His hand cupped her as if she had been made to fit his palm, his thumb stroking her nipple with a delicate, rhythmic intensity that brought a small, choked whimper from her throat.

Her body was slackening in his arms, turning boneless as tiny rivers of fire lapped at her nerve-endings, sapping any last thought of resistance.

He bent his head, and she felt the moist flame of his mouth against her inflamed skin, encompassing her, laving the aroused peak to new heights of sensation.

When his lips returned to hers, she welcomed him with passionate eagerness, her arm sliding up round his neck, her hand entwining in his hair to hold him closer yet.

His fingers fondled the curve of her hip, then glided downwards, and she was aware of a sudden, scalding rush of heat between her thighs as her startled flesh responded to the sureness of his touch.

His hand went to the fastening of her jeans, and paused...

He lifted his head, staring down at her, the blue eyes dazed and smoky, his breathing as ragged as her own.

'God, Chessie.' The words were slurred, dragged from his throat. 'What are you doing to me?' He shook his head in a kind of self-derision. 'All the times we've been alone together in this house—and I have to choose now—when my sister could walk in on us at any moment.'

It was reality with a vengeance. And it awoke Chessie to the horrified realisation of exactly what she'd invited.

Gasping, she jerked upright, hands shaking as she tried unavailingly to remedy the disarray in her clothing, and crawl away from him at the same time.

'Let me...'

'No.' She choked the word. 'Don't touch me. Don't dare…'

There was an incredulous silence, then, to her eternal mortification, Miles began to laugh softly.

'Why, Francesca,' he mocked, 'and you said you weren't a hypocrite.'

He got slowly to his feet, and stood, leaning against the arm of the Chesterfield as he watched her.

Knowing that he was nowhere as cool as he looked was no consolation for the total shamelessness of her behaviour either.

And she'd wanted him to go on, Chessie thought wildly as she dragged the edges of her shirt together. Wanted to be naked in his arms, and to give him whatever he asked.

Only that was impossible. Because, no matter how deep her need, the time would soon come when she would have to walk away. And she wanted to be able to do that with her head high, and her pride undamaged.

So, while she remained here in this house, even the slightest physical contact between them had to be strictly taboo from now on.

He said quite gently, 'I'm sorry.'

'I should hope you are,' she flung at him. 'You had no right…'

'You don't understand.' He cut across her. 'I'm sorry only for starting something I didn't finish. That was wrong of me.'

'Everything that happened here was wrong.' Her voice was suffocated. 'But it will never happen again—do you hear me? Otherwise I'm leaving, and to hell with four weeks' notice.'

His brows lifted. 'Do you really need to play the out-raged virgin?' he drawled coldly. 'I can't be the first—'

He stopped abruptly, his eyes narrowing suddenly as they studied her flushed embarrassment. Her averted gaze.

He said in a different voice, 'But I am the first, aren't I,

Francesca? So how can that be when you spent a summer with Alastair Markham?'

She lifted her chin. 'Perhaps he had too much respect for me to involve me in casual sex.'

'Is that what you think I was doing just now?' His smile was sardonic. 'Lady, believe me, I was in deadly earnest. And I still am. Because some time soon, despite all your protests, I intend to take you to bed.'

'You flatter me.' Her voice shook, mainly with anger, and that was good. She needed to sustain that anger, use it as a shield against him. Against the knowledge that if he crooked his little finger, she would walk over red-hot coals to him.

And that in spite of the fact that less than twelve hours ago he'd been making love to another woman. Oh, God, how pathetic was it possible to get? And how had she dared censure Jenny when she was equally bad?

She lifted her chin. 'However, I do not intend to be another notch on the bedpost in your—sexual rehabilitation.'

'Meaning?' She'd expected an angry, even explosive response, yet Miles sounded almost amused.

She said with emphasis, 'Meaning—I—will—not sleep with you.'

'Ah,' he said softly. 'But who mentioned sleeping?' He looked at her, and smiled, and for one shocked moment she felt as if he'd stripped all the clothes from her body.

Then he turned and went back to his table, and picked up the sheaf of correspondence lying there.

He said, without looking at her, 'If you're back to being the housekeeper, Chessie, then perhaps you should serve tea.'

She said between her teeth, 'Very well,' and marched to the door. She managed not to slam it behind her, then stood for a moment, leaning weakly against the sturdy panels, her mind reeling.

Why, she asked herself in total bewilderment, had it taken her all this time to realise she was in love with him?

Because it was no sudden thing, and she knew it. Even though she would have probably denied it with her last breath, he had been necessary to her for a long time. And she had hidden behind the barrier of their working relationship, and told herself it was enough.

But I lied, she thought desolately. And now there's nothing left for me but to go on lying.

As she straightened she looked down at herself in sudden dismay, recommencing the struggle to force her shirt buttons back into the relevant holes. She heard a faint noise, and, looking up, saw Steffie poised halfway down the stairs.

'Oh, no,' Chessie moaned under her breath as embarrassed heat swamped her again, and her already clumsy fingers turned into thumbs.

'Oh, dear,' Steffie commented with unabashed amusement. 'I quite forgot to sing.' And, her smile widening, she launched herself into a soft contralto rendering of Marvin Gaye's 'Sexual Healing'.

While Chessie swallowed back the tears threatening to engulf her, nailed on a smile of her own—and tried very hard to share the joke.

CHAPTER EIGHT

ENCOUNTERING Steffie had probably been the best thing that could have happened to her, Chessie decided that night, when she could at last escape to her own part of the house. Otherwise, she would probably have served tea with very red eyes, thus alerting Miles to her emotional state. Which was the last thing she wanted.

On the other hand, Miles' sister was so friendly, and genuinely eager to welcome her to the family, that Chessie felt even more guilty over the deception she was perpetrating.

But guilt was probably easier to deal with than her agony of confusion over Miles.

No matter how professional she'd intended their relationship to be, and how aloof she'd vowed to remain, there had always been pitfalls to living in the same house with a man as dynamic as Miles Hunter. It hadn't been easy, because he could be tricky, but it had never been less than fascinating, throwing up new challenges all the time.

Proximity, she thought wearily, has a lot to answer for.

And, maybe, at the beginning, gratitude had played its part too. Because there was no denying he'd provided her with a roof, a livelihood, and a form of security, even if it was for his own convenience.

There was also, she supposed, the glamour of his status as a best-selling writer, although she knew in her heart it had always been Miles the man she'd been drawn to—and not for purely intellectual reasons either. Because if she'd merely glimpsed him at some social gathering, with no idea who he was, she knew she would have looked—and looked again.

No amount of scarring could diminish his physical attraction in the least, she thought, and Sandie Wells had been worse than an idiot to walk away from him.

All of this an undeniably potent mix for a girl who had as little experience of men as herself.

And small wonder she was lying awake again, wondering what to do next and failing to come up with any answers.

Oh, if I could just turn the clock back, she thought unhappily. I'd have been happy to go on typing and cooking, and never asked for more.

Yet now it was as if someone had opened a door in a high wall, and shown her paradise, and there was no going back to her earlier innocence. Not when she knew what it was to be in Miles' arms and to discover the ravishment of his hands and lips on her body.

Just the memory of that was enough to send a shiver of longing rippling through her senses.

But it could not reconcile her to the prospect of a marriage without real love in it, she thought sadly. And that was all he'd offered, however practised he might be in the art of giving physical pleasure.

She didn't know what he'd been like before his accident, but now there seemed to be a cold core in Miles that she could not reach, and which might explain why romance had no place in his novels.

He doesn't think it matters, she told herself, and that applies to his life as well as his literature. But it matters to me.

He'd called her his 'sweet love', but that was only the language of seduction. He wanted to take her to bed. He'd said so quite openly. It went no deeper than that and perhaps Linnet's cynical advice years ago hadn't been so far off the mark after all.

She turned over, burying her face in her pillow. It would be easier tomorrow, she thought. Miles was taking Steffie sightseeing for the day, and although she'd been invited to go with them she'd refused, inventing an endless list of weekend chores. Miles had given her a thoughtful look, but he hadn't pressed her.

And in the evening, she had the ordeal of dinner at the Court to face, and that was something she couldn't get out of.

Steffie had mentioned it over the evening meal. 'Who are these Markhams, love?' she'd asked Miles. 'And will I like them?'

He'd shrugged, his face inscrutable. 'You'd better ask Francesca,' he commented indifferently. 'They're her friends, rather than mine. I've only just made their acquaintance. And I've never met Sir Robert Markham, or his son, come to that. At least, not officially.'

'I doubt that you'll meet Sir Robert tomorrow either,' Chessie said, biting her lip. 'He's had a severe stroke,' she added to Steffie. 'And he's now in a wheelchair. I don't think he'll be well enough to see people, or that he'd even want to.'

There was an odd, rather strained silence. Then Steffie said quietly, 'I see. How terrible for him, poor man. And for his family, of course.'

Miles' smile was a little remote. 'I think Lady Markham is bearing up in spite of everything—don't you, darling?'

'She has great strength of character,' Chessie agreed evenly. *And not a great deal of choice*, she added under her breath. She reached for the serving dish. 'Would anyone like any more beef?'

Looking back, she was faintly bewildered by the exchange. Did Steffie think she'd been tactless, referring to Sir Robert's physical disability in front of Miles? Had she unwittingly revived bitter memories of the way he used to be?

Surely there was no comparison between their two situations, she thought. Miles might use a walking stick, but he could walk wherever he wanted, drive a car—and make love to any woman who took his fancy, it seemed. Whereas Sir Robert was paralysed, and might remain so.

Besides, Miles could always have refused Linnet's invitation.

Oh, how I wish he had, she thought. For all kinds of reasons.

She was still wishing the same thing the following evening as she changed into one of the new dresses she'd bought in Hurstleigh. It was in a fine silky fabric, patterned with tiny cream daisies on a dark green background, sleeveless and round-necked, with a brief swirl of a skirt falling to just below her knee.

It was the first completely frivolous thing she'd bought in a long time, and she hardly recognised herself as she circled slowly in front of the mirror. But it wasn't just the dress, she thought. Suddenly, she was a girl with secrets in her eyes.

In the back of the wardrobe she found some cream strappy sandals and a matching bag. Relics of her former life. And from the bottom of a drawer, she unearthed a cream shawl with a long fringe, and draped it round her shoulders.

Ready, she told herself, for anything the next few hours might throw at her.

'You look lovely,' Steffie approved, herself elegant in black, when she joined brother and sister in the drawing room. 'Doesn't she, Miles?'

'Quite breathtaking. Have I seen that dress before?'

Chessie shook her head. 'I bought it the other day,' she said. 'In Hurstleigh'

'An eventful trip.' His smile did not reach his eyes.

'And clearly a successful one,' Steffie contributed cheerfully. 'There are no decent clothes shops where I live. When I need something I have to trail up to London.'

She carried on the same line of insouciant chatter on the short drive to the Court, and Chessie was glad of it as she sat silently beside Miles, acutely, almost shamingly aware of him.

The big house was lit up like a Christmas tree. They were admitted by Mrs Cummings, wearing the smart navy uniform that Linnet had always insisted on. And the lady of the house was waiting in the doorway of the drawing room, all smiles. She was wearing another of her figure-hugging dresses in deep crimson jersey, with lips and nails to match.

She looked, Chessie decided dispassionately, like some exotic jungle flower. One of the poisonous variety.

'Miles—so wonderful to see you.' The words poured out like warm treacle. 'And this is your sister, Mrs Barnes? Except that's so formal. Do let's make it Stephanie and Linnet. Oh, Chessie,' she added as an afterthought. 'Good evening. If you're looking for Alastair, he's with his father.'

I wasn't, Chessie thought indignantly. Aloud, she said quietly, 'How is Sir Robert?'

'I'm told he's making progress.' Linnet shrugged. 'I can't see any sign of it, myself. But his nurse seems very good.' She turned to the others. 'The big problem is he's incapable of dealing with his affairs at the moment, and there's no power of attorney. The lawyers are having to set up some emergency procedure, but it takes time, and it's so inconvenient.'

She might have been talking about the cancellation of a hairdressing appointment, Chessie reflected with distaste.

Linnet was targeting her again. 'Why don't you run over to the West Wing, sweetie, and tell Alastair the guests are here? After all, you know the way. You'll find him in the Blue Room.'

Which immediately established her in the same bracket as Mrs Cummings, whose task it should have been, Chessie realised with shock. For her hostess, her smart new dress and the ring on her finger counted for nothing. She was primarily Miles' housekeeper.

She said in a small stony voice, 'Yes—of course.' And left the room.

She was quivering with temper as she went towards the Blue Room, but she made herself calm down. She'd read somewhere that stroke patients needed a tranquil atmosphere, so she didn't want to carry her resentment of Linnet's cavalier behaviour into Sir Robert's sick room.

As she reached the door it opened, and a middle-aged woman in a nurse's uniform emerged carrying a tray covered by a white cloth. She checked when she saw Chessie. 'Can I help you?' She spoke briskly, her eyes shrewd behind her glasses.

'I'm Francesca Lloyd,' Chessie said quietly. 'A—a friend of the family. Lady Markham sent me to fetch her stepson.'

'Chessie?' Alastair's voice was raised questioningly. 'Come in.'

She drew a deep breath, and obeyed.

She was prepared for a shock, but she hadn't bargained for the ruined figure slumped in his wheelchair that confronted her. He was, she thought, barely recognisable, and for a moment dismay halted her, then she made herself smile and walk forward.

'Father.' Alastair bent over him. 'Here's Chessie to see you—Chessie Lloyd.'

She said quietly, 'Good evening, Sir Robert. I don't know if you remember me?'

The sunken eyes stared up at her with puzzled fierceness, then a spark of recognition seemed to dawn, and the sagging mouth struggled to utter a few guttural sounds. Chessie pulled forward a chair and sat down, putting a hand gently over Sir Robert's flaccid fingers. 'It's good to have you back. The village has missed you.'

She launched into a flow of gentle, almost inconsequential chat about what had been going on locally while he'd been in Spain, aware that his eyes were fixed on her face painfully, almost angrily.

Eventually Alastair broke in, a note of impatience in his tone. 'Isn't it time we were going in to dinner, Chessie?'

She glanced up, a little startled. 'Well, yes, but...'

'But Nurse Taylor is waiting to settle my father down

for the night. Besides, he doesn't understand a word you're saying,' he added with a shrug.

'You can't know that,' Chessie objected. She turned back to Sir Robert, and squeezed his hand. 'I hope you'll let me come back and see you again very soon,' she told him softly.

As she followed Alastair to the door she turned back, lifting her hand in farewell, and realised the sick man's gaze was still fixed on her, almost as if he was silently pleading with her. Or was she just being fanciful?

She smiled at Nurse Taylor who was waiting impassively. 'I'm sorry if I've interrupted your routine.'

'Please don't apologise. I'm sure it's done him good,' the older woman returned. She lowered her voice. 'And you're quite right. He understands far more than people credit,' she added, casting a significant glance at Alastair's retreating figure.

As Chessie joined him Alastair sent her a faintly derisive look. 'I never took you for Florence Nightingale, my sweet. Is this something you've learned from coping with your fiancé?'

She stared at him with frank distaste. 'That's a thoroughly unpleasant suggestion. What on earth's happening to you, Alastair?'

He shrugged defensively. 'Sorry, Chess, I'm just a bit wound up. To be honest, bringing Dad back here isn't working—for any of us.'

'But I thought this was where he wanted to be.'

'That was before he had the second stroke.'

'Oh.' Chessie shook her head. 'I didn't realise there'd been more than one.' She halted, gesturing round her. 'But surely being in his own environment again—back in the house he loves…'

'I'm not convinced he knows where he is, whatever that nurse says,' Alastair said moodily. 'After all, it's her job to boost his chances. Where there's life, there's hope and all that.'

'But people do make amazing recoveries…'

'Yes, but at what cost?' he demanded, impatient again. 'This house is a dinosaur. It eats money. And Dad's had so many chances to sell it, even before he went to Spain. A hotel chain were after it, and one of the private health companies, as well as property developers. It has to go, and as far as I'm concerned it should be sooner rather than later. Just as soon as I get control of my father's affairs, in fact.'

'But it's your family home,' Chessie protested. 'There have been Markhams here for generations.'

'Well, here's a Markham that has very different plans.' He saw her white face, the sudden tears in her eyes, and softened his tone. 'Chessie, my father would be far better off in a good nursing home. You must see that.'

'Would he?' she asked bitterly. 'All I can think about is how he'd hate to know these decisions were being made for him. In spite of him, even.' There was a choke in her voice. 'I remember what he was like—before. The way he'd stride about, giving his orders. He was so strong, so full of life, and now he's totally helpless in that ghastly chair—and it's so *awful*,' she added passionately. 'I—I can't bear seeing him like that.'

Alastair put his arms around her, drawing her forward to lean against his shoulder. 'Poor Chess,' he muttered. 'But it's terrible for me, too, you know. And I have to decide what's best for everyone.'

For everyone? Chessie wondered. Or for yourself—and Linnet…

Distressed as she was, she experienced a sudden uneasy prickle of awareness. Looking round, she saw Miles standing at the end of the corridor, leaning on his cane. He was watching them, his face expressionless.

'Oh.' She detached herself hurriedly, aware that she was blushing. 'Alastair—you haven't actually met my fiancé, Miles Hunter.' Her words seemed to tumble over themselves. 'Miles, this is Alastair Markham.'

Miles limped forward, extending his hand. 'How do you

do?' he said with cool politeness. 'Lady Markham wanted you to know that dinner is served.'

'Oh, dear. Have we kept you all waiting?' Alastair smiled with easy charm. 'But Chessie and I had things to talk over.' He gave her a swift, almost caressing smile. 'I'd better go and grovel to Stepmother.'

He disappeared, leaving Chessie and Miles alone together.

There was a taut silence. Then: 'That,' Chessie said in a fierce whisper, 'was *not* what you think.'

'Unless you've become a mind-reader,' Miles drawled scornfully, 'you can't possibly know what I think.'

'I can make an educated guess,' she flung back at him. 'But you're wrong. His father's in a bad way, almost completely paralysed, and I was upset, that's all.' She dragged a hand across her damp cheeks. 'I just wasn't prepared— not when I remember how things used to be...' she added in a muffled voice.

'I'm sorry,' Miles said quietly, after a lengthy pause. 'It can't be easy for you.'

'I'll survive.' She lifted her chin, forcing a smile. 'Now I'd better do something about my face.' And she walked quickly away.

The meal that followed did little to raise her spirits. Linnet dominated the conversation, talking with open discontent about the wonderful life she'd been forced to abandon in Spain, and how she couldn't wait to return.

Which would happen, Chessie supposed bitterly, when Wenmore Court was sold to the highest bidder, and Sir Robert was safely hidden away in some private facility.

She sighed quietly, then looked up to find Miles' reflective gaze fixed on her. She offered him a tentative smile, but it was not returned. Instead he turned to Linnet with some bread and butter question about the Spanish property market.

She bit her lip, then switched her attention to Alastair. 'Is the Midsummer Party still going ahead?'

He offered her more wine, and, when she declined, filled his own glass. 'We thought we'd give it a whirl,' he agreed carelessly. 'Go out on a high note. There isn't time to organise the usual full-scale fête, of course. So it will just be the evening party.'

To which I was never invited, Chessie thought.

'Which reminds me,' Linnet broke in. She gave Miles a seductive smile, making great play with her eyelashes. 'As the party's for charity, I thought it would be fun to have a celebrity speaker during supper. Just ten minutes' light chat about past career and future plans, you know the kind of thing. And you'd be ideal.' She put a coaxing hand on his arm. 'So you will be a darling, and help us out, won't you?'

'I'm afraid not,' Miles returned, unmoved. 'I'll gladly make a donation, but I don't do public appearances.'

'But you've no need to feel self-conscious,' Linnet purred. 'And nearly everyone there will be local, so they'll understand, anyway.'

Chessie found she was holding her breath, but Miles was imperturbable.

'Thank you for being so reassuring,' he said, 'but my answer still has to be "no".' He paused. 'For one thing, I'm not sure what my plans will be around that time.'

'Oh, well.' Linnet gave a fatalistic shrug. 'I'll have to think of something else. Unless of course you were sweet enough to change your mind,' she added with another dazzling smile. 'But I suppose that's too much to hope for.'

'I'm convinced of it,' Miles said gently, and changed the subject.

Leaving Chessie to ponder exactly what those plans he'd referred to might be...

'Did you say these people were friends of yours?' Steffie enquired caustically.

Dinner was over, and Linnet had swept both her female guests up to her bedroom 'to freshen up' as she'd coyly put it. She'd left them there to their own devices, merely telling them that there would be coffee in the drawing room when they came down.

Chessie fiddled with her lipstick. 'Not exactly,' she returned reluctantly. 'The summer I left school, I spent some time with Alastair, that's all.'

Steffie's brows lifted. 'Really? Was it serious?'

'I thought so then. But it was just a boy/girl thing. It petered out when his father sent him to business school in America.' She hesitated. 'I don't actually think Sir Robert approved, anyway.'

'I see.' Steffie dabbed scent on her wrists. Her voice was level. 'And is that why you were gone for such ages before dinner—because you were catching up on old times?'

'No, of course not. I was trying to talk to Sir Robert.' She shook her head. 'He seemed to know who I was, but it wasn't easy. He can't move—or speak.'

Steffie was silent for a long moment, then she said quietly, 'That—does not bear thinking about. Poor man.'

She sighed abruptly, then determinedly took herself in hand. 'So what about the glamorous Lady Markham, then?' She glanced round her surroundings with unholy appreciation. 'I suppose this is what they mean by a boudoir. I love the curtained bed and fluffy rugs—just like an old-fashioned Hollywood film set. I keep expecting someone to shout "Camera! Action!"' She chuckled. 'The tub for two in the *en suite* bathroom is fairly special, as well.' She paused, thoughtfully. 'I wonder who shares it with her.'

'I suppose Sir Robert used to.' Chessie tried to visualise this, and failed. In fact, she couldn't imagine him forging a path through the bedroom's floating draperies either.

Steffie put her scent back in her bag, and closed it. 'Did you tell Miles how bad he was?' Her tone was over-casual.

'I didn't really have a choice. He could see I was upset.' Chessie gave her a puzzled look. 'Why do you ask?'

Steffie sighed again. 'It's just that it could have stirred up a hornet's nest for him.' She hesitated. 'Has he told you why he still walks with a limp?'

'He rarely mentions any of it.'

'After the incident, they had to operate to remove steel fragments, and the X-rays showed one piece embedded near his spine.' Steffie's face relived the nightmare. 'He was told that removing it was not going to be easy, and that even if they succeeded there was a fifty-fifty chance that he'd be left paralysed.'

She shuddered. 'It was a ghastly possibility, and he was emotionally shattered anyway, while Sandie was having hysterics all over the place, so—he told them not to risk it.' She gave Chessie a wan smile. 'But it's still a sensitive topic.'

'Yes,' Chessie said slowly. 'I—I can see it would be. I'm glad you told me.'

'However, it's well in the past,' Steffie continued more robustly. 'And now he has the future to look forward to—with you. So no need to raise it, really—unless he does.'

No, Chessie thought as she followed her downstairs. No need at all.

She couldn't wait for the evening to be over, but it seemed to drag on for ever. In the drawing room, she found that Linnet had stationed herself next to Miles on one of the sofas, and embarked on the kind of murmured conversation that required her to lean intimately towards him, and touch his arm a lot.

Alastair, looking moody, was fiddling with the small pile of sheet music on top of the grand piano.

'Chessie—do you remember this?' He'd picked up one of the pieces, and was beckoning to her. Reluctantly she went over to him. 'It's that duet we used to play.' He smiled at her coaxingly. 'Shall we try it out again?'

'Oh, no,' she protested. 'I—I haven't played the piano in years. I really can't...'

'Of course you can.' He was arranging the music on the stand, placing the piano stool correctly. 'Come on, it'll be fun.'

'Yes, why not?' Steffie urged, smiling. 'Did you know your fiancée could play the piano, Miles?'

His smile was cool, almost cynical. 'No, but then Chessie has so many little secrets.'

Biting her lip, she joined Alastair on the piano stool. It was the kind of bravura piece that sounded more difficult than it actually was, and after a nervous start she acquitted herself well.

'There you are.' Alastair gave her a lingering smile as the others applauded. 'Perfect harmony.'

Chessie wanted to scream.

'Well, that was a barrel of laughs,' Steffie observed as the car made its way down the drive at last. 'Lady Markham was paying you a lot of attention, brother dear. Practising for when she's a merry widow?'

'I don't think she needs to.' Miles' tone was sardonic. 'I'd say her plans are already made.'

When they reached Silvertrees, Steffie excused herself almost immediately, and went to bed. 'Too much excitement is bad for me,' she explained.

'And what about you, Francesca?' Miles said softly when she'd gone. 'Are you going to be too excited to sleep tonight?'

'Why should I be?'

He shrugged. 'You had quite an eventful time. That was—a virtuoso performance you gave.'

'My piano playing has never been more than mediocre,' she denied curtly.

'Ah,' he said. 'But perhaps I wasn't talking about the duet.'

'Then say what you really mean.' Chessie rounded on him with sudden fierceness. 'Because I've had it up to here tonight. I was snubbed by that bitch,' she went on hotly. 'I had to watch someone I once respected suffering and helpless. And to cap it all, the Court's going to be sold off—

as ghastly flats or something—and—and they're all going
to leave…'

And, to her own surprise, she burst into tears.

Miles said wearily, 'Oh, dear God.' He led her over to
a sofa, made her sit, pressed an immaculate handkerchief
into her hand, and brought her a glass of brandy as she sat,
hiccuping, her eyes streaming.

'No, drink it,' he directed as she tried to demur.

She wanted him to sit beside her so that she could throw
herself into his arms and weep all down his shirt, but he
took a seat on the sofa opposite instead.

After a while, he said, 'You really care, don't you?'

'I didn't think so.' She drank some of the brandy. 'But
I suppose I must.'

How can I explain, she thought, that Sir Robert's face
doesn't belong to him any more, and his clothes all seem
too big as if he's shrunk? And instead of being the master
in his own house, he's just a nuisance that they'll shunt
into a home and forget, because Linnet wants to go back
to Spain, and Alastair's got a job in the City, and they're
both vile and shallow.

And, worst of all, how I keep thinking that it could be
you in that wheelchair, unable to move. You—my dear
love…

And that is the unbearable thing. Which I cannot tell you
because I'm not supposed to know.

She put down the glass. 'I'm sorry. I've behaved like an
idiot. I—I'll go to bed now.'

She rose, and Miles got to his feet too.

He said, 'Goodnight, Francesca. I hope you sleep well.'

She looked across at him, and everything she felt for
him—all that she longed for and desired to give—roared
through her suddenly like a flood-tide. Carrying her away…

And she heard her own voice saying, 'May I sleep with
you tonight?'

There was a silence, then he said quietly, 'No, that
wouldn't be a good idea.'

She tried to smile, but it turned into a grimace instead. 'Don't you—want me?'

'Yes,' he said. 'Far too much, indeed, to offer you the kind of comfort you seem to need tonight.'

'It isn't that...'

'No?' His brows lifted. 'Frankly, I don't think you know how you feel.' He paused. 'I'm not a saint, Francesca, nor am I in the mood for the initiation of an inexperienced girl. My needs, this evening, are very different. I don't think I could handle the inevitable aftermath, either,' he added drily. 'Believe me, things are best left as they are.'

'Yes,' she said. 'I—I'm sorry.' His handkerchief was a damp ball, crushed in her hand. She felt numb now, but soon the pain would begin, and for that she needed to be alone. Because she could not let him see...

She looked at him, her lips moving in a small, meaningless smile. 'Well—goodnight.'

I have to get out of here, she thought. *I have to get out before I fall on my knees and beg him to take me, here on the floor.*

'Chessie.' His voice was suddenly husky. 'Listen—I want you to understand...'

'I do,' she said. 'Really. You don't need to explain any more. And I'll try not to embarrass you again.'

Walking away was easy, she discovered. Just a matter of putting one foot in front of another until, somehow, she reached the door, and could close it behind her.

And then, one clenched fist bruising her lips, she ran.

CHAPTER NINE

ON ANY normal Sunday, Chessie could have avoided Miles, of course, because it was part of her jealously guarded free time. But Steffie's presence changed everything. So, she would have to come out of hiding, and make coffee, and cook lunch, and say goodbye at some point in the afternoon—and pretend all the while that she weren't dying inside.

She had no idea how she was going to face Miles, as she would soon have to do. She had fled from him the previous night, humiliated beyond belief, and had spent much of the night pacing round her small sitting room, trying to come to terms with what had happened.

In a strange way, it was his kindness that had hit her the hardest. He had obviously been trying to let her down gently.

But would it really have made her feel any better if he'd told her with brutal honesty that his sexual needs were being satisfied elsewhere by an infinitely more sophisticated partner?

Just the thought was enough to send her anguished mind wincing into limbo.

But before she'd allowed her tired body and reeling mind to sleep last night, she'd managed to make a few big decisions.

And the first and most important was that she would never make such a fool of herself again. Never again be a suppliant to a man who had nothing to give. In that way, she might be able to salvage a few rags of pride.

In addition, whatever job she took would only be temporary, she told herself. As soon as Jenny started college, she would start again too. Go right away somewhere—maybe abroad, and forge a whole new life for herself.

And teach herself to forget the old one.

It would not be easy. Every time she walked past a bookstand anywhere in the world, she'd probably see Miles Hunter's name emblazoned there. And memory of this brief time would claw at her again.

But slowly—gradually—she would become accustomed. Even hardened. And then one day, far in the future, she would cease to care at all.

She dusted and vacuumed the flat, then showered and changed into her navy skirt and a matching short-sleeved top. She pulled her newly washed hair back from her face, and confined it at the nape of her neck with a silver clasp.

This was the image she would present from now on—businesslike and practical. And aloof.

When she reached the main house, she found the study door was firmly shut, and from behind it she heard the staccato rattle of typewriter keys.

Steffie was stretched out on one of the drawing room sofas with the Sunday papers spread around her.

'I thought Sunday was supposed to be a day of rest,' she complained languidly. 'Yet my dear brother was down here at dawn, giving that machine of his serious grief.'

'He's at a critical point in the book,' Chessie offered rather lamely.

'Really?' Steffie's smile was catlike. 'Now I'd attributed it to a totally different cause.' She gave Chessie a shrewd look. 'Did you two have a fight last night?'

Chessie bit her lip. 'Absolutely not.'

'You didn't take exception to Miss Deadly Nightshade 1980 coming on to him last night? And he didn't comment on the amount of attention the boy tycoon was paying you in return?' Steffie cast her eyes to the ceiling. 'I thought there'd be blood on the carpet this morning.'

'I've known the Markhams a long time,' Chessie said. 'And Miles—understands that.'

'Does he?' Steffie's voice was tart. 'Then he must have developed powers of tolerance that I've never suspected.'

'Well, we all change.' Chessie gave her a brief, brittle smile. 'Would you like your coffee served in here?'

'In other words—mind my own business.' Steffie swung her legs off the sofa. 'But I'll come along to the kitchen, if that's all right. The amazingly understanding Miles doesn't wish to be disturbed, and I can lend a hand with lunch.'

She gave Chessie a companionable pat on the shoulder. 'And don't look so worried, sugar. The inquisition is over for the day.'

She was as good as her word. In the kitchen, she was deft and competent, chatting about recipes, and the problems of cooking for a family none of whom seemed to like the same food.

'I'm not in the way, am I?' she broke off at one point to enquire.

'No—really.' Chessie hastened to assure her. She smiled. 'It's such a novelty, having someone to chat with while I'm cooking.'

'Not your sister?'

'Heavens, no.' Chessie pulled a face. 'You'd never find Jenny within a mile of a stove.' She shook her head. 'I don't know how she'll cope when she goes to college.'

'I have news for you,' Steffie told her solemnly. 'Very few students die of starvation—even in the first year.' She paused. 'Isn't she joining us for lunch?'

'She's gone to a friend's house for some last-ditch revision. Her exams start tomorrow.' At least that was what Chessie hoped she was doing. Any mention of Zak Woods had become taboo.

It would be good to confide in Steffie and ask her advice, but also pointless as they were unlikely to meet again.

Life could be very unfair, Chessie thought ruefully, scraping carrots. Just as she'd found a woman she'd have liked as a friend, she was about to lose her again.

'Well, I think a glass of sherry is called for,' Steffie commented with satisfaction as lunchtime approached.

'Not for me, thanks,' Chessie said quickly. 'Perhaps you'd tell Miles that everything's ready while I dish up.'

She'd made a creamy cauliflower soup, to be followed by roast beef and Yorkshire pudding, and a lemon meringue pie was waiting on its serving dish. It all looked and smelled wonderful, and she wouldn't care if another morsel of food never passed her lips.

From the doorway, Miles said softly, 'Running away again, Francesca?'

She did not look round. Her voice taut, she said, 'I'm serving lunch. That's what happens when you have a guest. And I am the housekeeper.'

'To hell with lunch. We need to talk.'

'About last night?' She concentrated fiercely on stirring the soup. 'There's nothing to discuss.'

'I think there is.' His voice gentled. 'I want to explain...'

'No.' She almost slammed down the spoon. 'I don't want your explanations—or your sympathy. I'm not the first person to find herself in love with the wrong man. It happens.' She shrugged. 'I'll get over it.'

'You do realise, then, that it can't work?' He sounded almost surprised. 'You've accepted that—in spite of everything?'

'Yes, of course.' She took a bowl from the warming oven, and poured the soup into it. 'But last night had nothing to do with it. I—found out some time ago.'

'I was afraid you'd be hurt,' he said quietly. 'And you are. I shall always regret that. But remember this, Francesca, you need never settle for second-best.'

'Advice to treasure.' She turned a brief glittering smile on him. 'Now perhaps you'd take Steffie into the dining room. Unless you have any more worldly wisdom to pass on, of course?'

Miles took a step towards her, and for a frantic moment she thought he was going to touch her, and knew that the

mere brush of his hand would be enough to destroy her—
to smash her into small, bleak fragments.

She said hoarsely, *'No'* and recoiled, her white face dar-
ing him to come any closer.

He stopped instantly, staring at her, his lips parting in
shock and disbelief.

He looked, she realised, almost haggard, and for a moment her heart lurched. Then she was back in control, loading the steaming bowl and the soup plates onto a tray.

In a voice that seemed to belong to someone else, she
said, 'If you'll take Stephanie into the dining room—
please…'

Without another word, he turned and limped away, leaving her to follow with the tray.

It was going to be one of the worst meals of her life, she
thought apprehensively as she ladled out the soup. Miles'
face looked as if it had been carved from granite. And she
herself felt as if she were balanced on a knife-edge.

She saw Stephanie give both of them a quick glance,
then launch airily into a series of reminiscences about her
working days. She too had been a journalist, Chessie discovered, but on various magazines rather than a newspaper,
and her verbal portraits of some of the celebrities she'd
interviewed were wickedly funny.

Even Miles' set expression had relaxed into a faint smile,
although he took little part in the conversation himself. But
then, under normal circumstances, he wouldn't have come
to lunch at all when he was working, Chessie reflected.
Instead, he'd have asked her to slice off some of the beef
and put it in a sandwich he could eat in his study.

She forced herself to eat, to offer second helpings, and
accept praise for her cooking. While inside she felt cold
and numb.

Because, presently, Steffie would be gone, and she would
be alone with Miles again.

And, as if on cue, Steffie glanced at her watch. 'It's time

I was leaving for the station, brother, dear, or my family will think I've been abducted by aliens.'

At the front door, she gave Chessie a fierce hug. 'I've told Miles, he must bring you to stay—meet the monsters on their home territory.' She paused, lowering her voice. 'And don't worry. Everything will work out, you'll see.'

Chessie stood in the doorway, waving goodbye as Miles' car moved down the drive, her face aching with the effort to smile.

Once the door was shut, she flew into action, clearing the table and loading the dishwasher. Tidying the dining room and returning the drawing room to its usual pristine elegance.

I have to be out of the house before Miles comes back. Have to…

The words ran in her head like some feverish mantra.

The clearing-up done, Chessie changed swiftly into jeans and a sweatshirt, and went quickly and quietly out of the rear gate, and up into the birch woods behind the house.

The sun glinted down on her through the slender branches, and she could hear the throaty murmurings of woodpigeons as she walked briskly, hands in pockets.

At the top of the rise, she turned and looked back, and saw the roof of the house through the sheltering trees.

There had been a time when to leave it behind would have been an unbearable wrench. Now, she could not wait to get away.

If only, she thought, her memories could so easily be left behind. But, like this ache in her heart, they would be with her always. Even, she realised with a kind of helpless desolation, if she went to the ends of the earth.

'They've had valuation people round at the Court.' Mrs Chubb wagged her head. 'Looks like Madam's planning to sell up.' She snorted. 'Scandalous, I call it. If Sir Robert had his health and strength, he'd soon give them their marching orders.'

'But he is getting better,' Chessie protested. 'Now that he's having regular physiotherapy, he's got movement back in his hand and arm. Only it's a slow process.'

'Too slow to save the Court, I reckon,' Mrs Chubb said ominously. 'And not everyone there is glad to see the gentleman improve either.'

'Mrs Chubb,' Chessie said uncomfortably, 'you really mustn't…'

'Mark my words,' the lady returned magisterially. 'That Nurse Taylor was saying the other day, he'd be hard up for visitors, his own flesh and blood included, but for you—and Mr Hunter, of course.'

Chessie, who was making coffee, nearly spilled boiling water on the stove. 'Miles visits Sir Robert?' she exclaimed, and could have kicked herself for betraying her astonishment.

Mrs Chubb nodded with satisfaction. 'Almost as regular as yourself. Reads the paper to him, and such.' She gave Chessie a shrewd look. 'He hasn't told you, then.'

Chessie put the coffee-pot on its stand. She said coolly, 'He probably mentioned it. But he doesn't have to account to me for every minute of his day, Mrs Chubb.'

Nor did he, she thought unhappily as she carried his coffee to the study a little while later.

They were right back to the early days of their working relationship, with Miles behind a barrier of aloof courtesy she found it impossible to breach. And telling herself over and over again that this was for the best did nothing to assuage the pain of it.

She sometimes wondered if the events of the past weeks had simply been a preposterous dream. But the ring that she still wore, at his brusque insistence, told her differently. And so did the ache in her heart.

Not that she was allowed a great deal of time for introspection, she admitted almost gratefully.

Miles was driving himself harder than ever to finish the current book—almost as if he were out to break some kind of record. And he was being incredibly tough on himself, too, making constant alterations and revisions. For the first time since she'd started working for him, Chessie was pushed to keep up.

But it wasn't all graft, she reminded herself with difficulty. Miles had paid another two visits to London, each time remaining overnight. So he was allowing himself some rest and recreation at least, even if she was left in sleepless torment, at the mercy of her too-vivid imagination.

As she reached the hall the front door bell sounded imperiously. She put the tray down on a side table and went to answer its summons. She was frankly taken aback to find Linnet waiting.

'Is Miles at home?' The older woman walked past her. 'Ah, I can see he is,' she added, spotting the coffee-pot and cups. 'Why don't I kill two birds with one stone and take this in for you?'

'But he's working,' Chessie intervened desperately. 'He really can't be interrupted.'

'Nonsense,' Linnet said lightly. 'You must try to be less possessive, my sweet.' And she opened the study door, and carried in the tray, Chessie trailing behind her apprehensively.

'Darling Miles...' Linnet's voice and smile were appealing '...Chessie seemed to think you were too busy to see me. Surely not.'

'I'm honoured.' Miles rose awkwardly, reaching for his cane. 'Bring another cup, will you, Francesca?'

'There are two on the tray,' Chessie said quietly. 'I'll have my coffee later.'

'Don't go, Chessie.' Linnet disposed herself gracefully on the Chesterfield. 'This concerns you too.' She produced a large square envelope from her bag, and handed it to Miles with a flourish. 'Your invitation to the summer party.'

'Thank you.' His brows lifted. 'Is the post office on strike?'

'Oh, I wanted to bring it in person—to make sure you're going to accept. I was saying to my stepson how little we've seen of you over the past couple of weeks. I hope you're not becoming a recluse.'

'On the contrary, I've been out a great deal—much of the time at the Court,' Miles returned silkily. 'However we seem to keep missing each other.'

For one joyous moment, Chessie saw Linnet actually disconcerted, but she soon recovered. 'What a shame, but of course I'm frantically busy with the arrangements for the party. Dashing here, there and everywhere. I've decided to have tombola during supper—but with more interesting prizes than the usual cans and bottles.'

She gave Miles an arch look. 'I hope I can persuade you to contribute this time. A signed copy of your latest book, perhaps?'

'Willingly. Would you like it now?' Miles returned courteously. He walked over to the shelf, and took down one of the hardbacks, scribbling his name on the flyleaf.

'Perfect.' Linnet gave him a honeyed smile as she accepted it. 'All I need now is someone fabulous to run the tombola for me.' She paused. 'And I was wondering about Sandie Wells.'

His face expressionless, Miles poured out the coffee and handed her a cup. 'It's your party,' he said. 'Do as you think best.'

Linnet sighed. 'I haven't seen her in ages, of course. I suppose she'll be trying to get her career back on track, poor sweet, now that her marriage is on the rocks.' She gave him a limpid look. 'Could you ask her for me, darling?'

Chessie realised she was holding her breath, her eyes fixed painfully on Miles' impassive face.

He said quietly, 'I think it would be far better if you approached Sandie through Jerry Constant, her agent.'

Linnet sighed again. 'Well—perhaps. But I haven't finally decided to ask her, of course. I may run the tombola myself, along with everything else.'

She pulled a little face. 'I'd forgotten what a chore this party is to organise,' she confided. 'And Mrs Cummings isn't being as helpful as she could be either.

'Which brings me to you, Chessie,' she went on, smiling. 'I was wondering if you'd lend me your housekeeping skills for the party, and take over some of the catering. Nothing too onerous, of course—mostly buffet fodder. I'll be able to give you the numbers in a couple of days.'

'I think you forget,' Miles said gently. 'Chessie is in my full-time employment.'

She twinkled charmingly. 'But she can't have all that much to do,' she objected. 'Because a little bird tells me she can't keep away from the Court either. So, if you could just loan her to me for a few hours...'

'Quite impossible, I'm afraid. If Chessie wishes to attend the party, it will be with me, as my fiancée.' He looked at Chessie, his brows lifting, a challenge in his blue eyes. 'Well, darling? Do you want to go?'

'Of course,' Chessie said quietly. 'I wouldn't miss it.'
Especially if Sandie Wells is going to be there...

Linnet was simply mischief-making. She was sure of it. And although Miles had given nothing away, it must have had some effect on him.

Was it news to him that his former love had ended her marriage—or had he known already?

Suddenly, Chessie found herself remembering those mysterious letters. The woman's voice on the phone at the London flat.

Was it—could it be possible that Sandie Wells was back in Miles' life again? And was he the reason Sandie's marriage was over?

However desperate she was to find out, Chessie knew she could never ask. And jealousy, dark and despicable, twisted inside her like the blade of a poisoned knife.

'Maybe the landlady at The White Hart could help out with the food instead,' Miles was suggesting blandly.

'At her prices?' Linnet asked with something of a snap. 'I don't think so. Our other expenses are incredibly heavy, now, with the fees these agency nurses charge, and all this physiotherapy that does no good at all.'

'I gather Nurse Taylor wouldn't agree with you,' Miles said drily. 'She's delighted with the progress your husband is making. And she should know,' he added. 'She's worked with Sir Philip Jacks at the Kensington Foundation, which deals with whole numbers of stroke patients in addition to its other services.'

There were angry spots of colour in Linnet's cheeks. 'Oh, she's highly qualified, no doubt. I just don't want her giving my poor Robert false hope.'

'No,' Miles said quietly. 'I agree that would be cruel. But I'd say she prefers to deal in even chances.' He paused. 'Was there anything else? Would you like some more coffee?'

'Oh, please don't let me keep you.' Linnet drained her cup, and put it down. 'I have a thousand things to do. See you next week at the party,' she added brightly.

Miles was studying the elaborately engraved card when Chessie returned having seen their unwanted guest off the premises.

He said, 'What exactly have we let ourselves in for?'

'Not a great deal.' Chessie bit her lip. 'It used to be a much more elaborate affair, with all the local organisations running stalls and sideshows in the grounds during the afternoon. But this time, it's just drinks and dancing in a marquee on the lawn, and supper, of course.'

'Which will not be provided by you.'

'No.' She hesitated. 'I wouldn't have minded helping, you know.'

'I think we've done quite enough for charity with the cost of this ticket.' He tossed it onto his table, then paused. 'Don't sell yourself short, Francesca,' he added curtly.

'You're not cheap labour.' He paused, giving her a meditative glance. 'How's the job hunt going, by the way?'

'Oh, there are a few possibilities,' Chessie said, waiting for her nose to grow six inches. 'It's just a question of choosing the one with the best prospects.'

She'd applied to two agencies offering residential posts only to be told categorically that she was far too young. The latest rejection letter had arrived that morning.

'I'm sure it is.' Miles spoke abstractedly. He was already sitting at his table, feeding a sheet of paper into the typewriter, his attention clearly elsewhere.

But was he thinking solely about work, or had more personal matters intruded?

Whatever, she could consider herself dismissed, she thought flatly as she removed the tray.

At the door, she paused, a thousand questions milling in her head.

As if aware of her gaze, he glanced round. 'Yes?' The question was curt—almost as if he was warning her off. Forbidding her to probe too deeply.

She found herself saying, 'I—I didn't realise you were visiting Sir Robert as well.'

'Why should you? I went originally to pay my respects, which I signally failed to do when we were there for dinner,' he added, his mouth tightening. 'It was time for the nurse's break, but no one turned up to relieve her, so I filled in.' He looked at her, brows raised. 'Is it a problem for you?'

'No,' she said. 'On the contrary.' *Considering what Steffie told me, I thought you might be the one having the difficulty.* 'It—it's kind of you.'

His lip curled. 'Well, don't sound so surprised, Francesca. I am capable of the odd selfless action. I even gave your sister a lift home from school yesterday.'

'She didn't mention it.' Chessie looked at him with misgiving. 'Was she all right?'

'She was preoccupied but polite. Something of an advance, you'll agree.'

'Yes.' She paused, brow furrowed. 'I don't think her exams are going too well.'

'And when they're over, is she going to revert to snarling and sulking?'

'I hope not,' Chessie said, encouraged by the fact he was smiling faintly. 'But I can't guarantee a thing.'

Back in the hall, she leaned against the door panels for a moment, waiting for her heartbeat to settle down again before she took the tray to the kitchen.

She was thankful he would never know how deeply she yearned to have the right to touch him—to kiss the tiredness from his eyes. And—the sadness too. That, she thought, most of all.

And how she wanted quite desperately to beg him not to go away again.

But that, she thought, would be crying for the moon. And, anyway, she would be the next to leave—if she could just find somewhere to go.

Leaving him free to do exactly as he wished, she thought, and felt the knifeblade turn again.

'I can't believe you've done this.' Jenny glared at her accusingly. 'You've actually made us homeless?'

'Not exactly.' Chessie tried to make the impossible sound reasonable. 'I've managed to find a bedsit in Hurstleigh. It's big enough for us both, but not very glamorous. But the landlady says she'll let us do some redecorating at our own expense.'

'Well, yippee.' Her sister's voice dripped with sarcasm. 'And how do we afford that—as you're giving up your job as well?'

Chessie hesitated. 'I'm going to be working at The White Hart on a temporary basis,' she said. 'The Fewstons need help with food preparation, and I'll do some waiting on tables as well.' She pinned on a smile. 'We'll manage.'

'Manage?' Jenny echoed derisively. 'Baby, you're out of your tree.'

No, thought Chessie with great weariness. Just at the end of my tether.

Aloud, she said, 'Jenny—it's all I could get. But it's not for ever.'

'You had this.' Jenny gestured round the flat. 'And you had The Ogre too. You were going to marry him, for God's sake. What's happened?'

Chessie hesitated. 'We—decided to call it off. So—I need to move on.'

A few terse words to encompass all the anguish, betrayal and heart-searching that had really gone on, she thought sadly.

'In other words, he's throwing us out. And just when I was beginning to think he might be semi-human after all,' Jenny said bitterly. 'But no. Lo and behold—he's a bastard.'

'No, he isn't.' Chessie was fierce. 'And I won't have you say that. It—it's a mutual decision. And you've always hated being here, anyway.'

'It's better than some slum in Hurstleigh, with you slaving in a pub for peanuts,' Jenny hit back. 'Well, don't expect me to go with you, Chess. I'm going to ask Linda's parents if I can stay with them. Linda's going to work, packing boxes at her father's factory during the holidays, and there's a job for me too if I want. I'm going to ring now, and tell them yes.'

And left Chessie sitting limply at the kitchen table with the sound of a slammed door ringing in her ears.

She got tiredly to her feet, and began to make herself some coffee. She'd always known that there'd be uproar when she finally told Jenny about the change in their circumstances, but there was simply no way she could conceal it any longer. Her time at Silvertrees was running out like the sand through an hourglass.

All this, she thought, and Linnet's damned party too.

She glanced through the kitchen window at the relentlessly blue sky, and wondered why it was that weather never seemed to reflect one's mood—or wishes. She'd prayed fervently for a monsoon, that would threaten to flood the giant marquee and force the whole thing to be called off. And, more importantly, ensure that she would not have to make her final public appearance as Miles' fiancée.

Her only consolation was the news, gleaned from Mrs Chubb, that their local MP's pretty red-haired daughter was running the tombola. So Sandie Wells was still just a few scraps of paper and a disembodied voice.

Maybe it would be better to see her face to face, she thought. Know your enemy.

She didn't have a clue what she was going to wear tonight. She supposed it would have to be the flowered dress again, although it wasn't really smart enough. And no doubt Linnet would recognise it instantly, and make some bitchy remark.

But that, she thought unhappily, was the least of her troubles.

Sandie Wells might not be present at the party, but Chessie was sure she was never far from Miles' thoughts. He'd been more than usually preoccupied during the last week, and it wasn't just the end of the book that was absorbing his attention. Clearly there were big decisions to be made—and ones he was not prepared to share with her.

Even the coffee tasted bitter today, and, grimacing, she poured it away and braced herself for the rest of the day.

She'd expected Miles to be working, finalising and refining the last chapter, but he was standing by the study window, deep in thought again, when she entered.

She said, 'I've brought the mail.'

'Leave it on the table.' He didn't look round. 'I'll deal with it later.'

She hesitated. 'You haven't forgotten it's the party at the Court tonight.'

Say you can't go, she willed him silently. Tell me you've still got too much work on the manuscript.

'On the contrary.' He dashed her hopes. 'I wouldn't miss it for the world either. And I have something for you.' He bent awkwardly, retrieving a large flat box that had been hidden behind his table.

'For me?' Chessie received it, startled. 'Do I open it?'

'Only if you want to see what's inside.'

Biting her lip, Chessie complied. Hidden inside the folds of tissue was a drift of creamy silk. She shook it free, and held it up, gasping a little. It was a dress, with narrow shoulder straps supporting a straight-cut bodice, which flowed down into a full-length gracefully fluted skirt. There was a matching jacket too, slender and reaching to her hips.

Miles said, 'It is your size. I checked with Jenny.'

For a long moment, she stared at the lovely thing, feeling her throat tighten uncontrollably, then quietly she replaced it in its sheltering tissue.

'You don't like it?'

She said in a low voice, 'It's beautiful—but I can't accept it.'

'Why not? Your notice hasn't run out yet, so we're still officially engaged, and we're making a very public appearance together tonight.' He shrugged. 'I thought your courage might need a boost. Or regard it as a uniform if that makes it easier.' His voice hardened. 'But you will wear it for me, Francesca, even if I have to dress you with my own hands, and that's an order.'

Her eyes snapped to his dark face in outrage—and sudden pleading. But there was no softening in the blue eyes.

'An order,' he repeated softly.

She replaced the lid on the box, and stepped back, tucking it under her arm.

'Very well—' her voice bit '—sir.' She paused. 'May I go now, please?'

He said grimly, 'I think you'd better—before you make me really angry. In fact, take the rest of the day off.' He limped to his table, and sat down. 'But be ready in the hall at eight, please,' he flung over his shoulder. 'And smile, darling, this evening. After all, you won't have many more of them to endure in my company.'

'No.' Chessie lifted her chin defiantly, hurting and wanting to hurt in return. 'And the sure and certain knowledge of that is all that makes—any of this—remotely bearable. Believe me, I'm counting the days.'

And she whirled, and almost ran from the study, banging the door behind her as she went.

CHAPTER TEN

To CHESSIE'S frustration, the dress looked even better when she was wearing it. She'd half-hoped it would either swim on her slender body, or be tight enough to rip, but it fitted perfectly, the skirt rippling round her ankles as she moved.

The only drawback was that its design forbade her to wear a bra, and, while this wasn't obvious, the cling of the bodice to her bare breasts made her feel absurdly self-conscious, and glad of the concealing jacket.

Earlier in the day, she'd rung the hairdresser in Hurstleigh where she went for her monthly trim, and arranged to have her hair highlighted, courtesy of a last-minute cancellation. She'd recklessly plunged on some new cosmetics too.

No one would think she looked like a robot tonight, she thought. She was all living, breathing woman. Although the wisdom of that was questionable.

She lingered for a moment in front of the mirror. The pale dress made her look almost bridal. And she fitted the old rhyme too. Her sandals were something old, and the dress something new. Blue, for the aquamarine on her finger. And borrowed—well, that was her remaining time with Miles.

But I'm going to a party, she reminded herself, shaking off the sudden feeling of bleakness that had assailed her. Probably my first and last for some time. And I intend to enjoy myself tonight—whatever the ultimate cost...

She gave herself a final, resolute smile, then left her room.

Jenny's door was ajar, but the room was empty, and a selection of her clothes, books and tapes was also missing.

It seemed she'd meant what she'd said, Chessie thought, biting her lip.

Her first impulse had been to take a taxi to Linda's house and insist that Jenny come home, but on second thoughts she'd decided it was best to let the situation calm down a little.

She would have to talk to Linda's mother, of course, if only to make sure that Jenny was really there, she thought, an unwanted image of Zak Woods imprinting itself on her mind. But, principally, she needed to know if the other woman was prepared to house Jenny for the time being, and, if so, offer to pay for her sister's keep until the packing job materialised. If it ever did.

It wasn't eight o'clock, yet Miles was already waiting, immaculate in dinner jacket and black tie. She'd never seen him in this kind of formal attire before, and her heart missed a beat.

She stood mutely, her face warming as his blue eyes performed a leisurely and detailed assessment of her in turn, from the glowing lights in her hair to the fluted hem of the skirt drifting round her ankles. Lingering, she was sure, on the thrust of her untrammelled breasts.

He said, quietly, 'You look—very lovely.'

The faint huskiness in his voice betrayed him, and her body responded with the swift flutter of her pulses, and the burgeoning, deep within her, of a soft, trembling ache.

For an endless moment, they stood, locked together in shaken, unacknowledged urgency. The space that separated them charged and tingling.

It was Miles who broke the spell.

He said, almost grimly, 'We'd better go.'

'Yes.' Her voice was barely a whisper. He'd remembered just in time, she thought as she followed him out of the house into the evening sunlight, why all connection between them had to be severed.

But she could understand why he'd insisted on maintaining the charade of their engagement. It was excellent camouflage while Sandie was obtaining her divorce.

It was all so simple when you worked it out. And Chessie had expended a lot of time and unhappiness in doing precisely that.

She sat beside him, in silence, her hands tightly clenched round her bag, telling herself it would be better—easier—when there were more people around them. That it was being alone with him that inflicted the lasting damage.

The lights in the huge marquee were already lit, and the sound of music drifted across the lawns as they approached.

Chessie found she was already bracing herself for her first encounter with Linnet, who was waiting at the entrance of the marquee to greet her arriving guests, handing out smiles like over-sweet bon-bons.

Tonight, she was sinuous in a strapless black satin creation that barely covered her full breasts, and flowed over every other inch of her like a second skin.

Chessie felt her eyes widening, and was needled to see that her companion was surveying his hostess with frank and totally male appreciation.

'Miles, darling, you're here at last,' she cooed. 'And Chessie. Still looking so virginal after all this time. How very sweet—and unexpected.'

Miles took Chessie's arm firmly and drew her away while she was still struggling to frame a suitable response.

'Yes, she's the arch bitch of the western world,' he said softly. 'But you don't have to join her in a slanging match. Regard what she said as a compliment. After all, I doubt if it's ever been used as an adjective about her.'

'Not in that dress at any rate,' Chessie, still smarting, said with something of snap. 'Not just no bra. No anything else, by the look of it.'

'And just how much more are you wearing, darling?' Miles murmured, his hand sliding down from her hip in a lightning exploration that forced a stunned gasp of outrage from her. 'A few inches of lace doesn't confer any moral superiority. In fact it can be even more enticing—under the right circumstances.' He smiled into her shocked eyes. 'Now come and have some champagne.'

'I bet no one ever applied "virgin" to you either,' Chessie said between her teeth as they walked to the bar set up along one side of the tent.

'Certainly not after the age of fifteen anyway,' he agreed without shame. 'Besides, wouldn't you rather go to bed with someone who knew what he was doing?'

Whatever she replied to that, she was on unsafe ground, and she knew it.

She said coldly, 'May we change the subject, please?'

'For now,' Miles told her pleasantly. 'But not for ever.'

Why? she thought. Why did he say things like that to her when he knew he didn't mean it? Why couldn't he limit the pretence to when other people were with them?

The chilled champagne felt wonderful against the dryness of her mouth, and she drank it far too quickly. Miles had her glass refilled, but chose mineral water for himself this time around.

'Don't you like champagne?' Chessie sipped the second glass with determined circumspection.

'Very much,' he said. 'But I'm driving.'

'We could always walk home,' she pointed out.

'I also want to keep a clear head.' He frowned slightly. 'I scent trouble.'

'You mean a fight?' Chessie tried for lightness, looking around her and shaking her head. 'I hardly think so. A lot of the top people in the county are here tonight.'

'Not that kind of trouble. I used to get bad vibes before certain assignments, always for good reason, warning me that something was wrong. And I have them now.'

Chessie stared into her glass. 'Did you get them before—that last one?'

He said softly, 'Oh, yes.'

'But you still went ahead with it?'

'Of course.'

'That,' Chessie said, 'was either extremely brave, or totally mad.'

'One doesn't necessarily rule out the other.' He paused. 'Someone's trying to catch your eye.'

Chessie glanced in the direction indicated, and stiffened. 'Heavens—Mrs Rankin. But she hasn't spoken to me since—well—in years...'

'Well, she seems determined to speak to you now,' Miles commented. 'She's coming over.'

And Mrs Rankin and her meek husband were only the first of many. Everyone suddenly wished to remember themselves to Chessie, and to meet her future husband, and, to her embarrassment, she found she was the centre of attention.

Although it was Miles they actually wanted to talk to, rather than herself, she reminded herself with cool realism. When word went round that she was no longer engaged to him, she would be consigned to oblivion again. Especially when it was discovered that she was waitressing at The White Hart.

When the disco started, there was almost a queue of men eager to ask her to dance. For a moment, she was hesitant, glancing at Miles, wondering how he would feel about her joining in an activity in which he could have no part.

But he only smiled and said lightly, 'Go for it, Chessie.'

She loved to dance, feeling the rhythm of the music in her bones. As she moved she was aware of Miles watching her from the edge of the floor, felt the intensity of his blue gaze like a hand on her bare skin. And she looked back at him, unable to disguise her longing for him, her lips trembling into a pantomime of a kiss. Only to see him turn away, and disappear into the crowd.

Her impulse was to run after him, but she managed to check herself. Why expose herself to further rejection? she thought bitterly. Far better to go on dancing with men who did want her company. And she smiled, and flirted, and let her body move seductively in the pale silk dress, and looked as if she didn't have a care in the world.

Her last partner, however, was more energetic than skilled, jigging around, red-faced as she swayed in front of him.

'Sorry, Greg.' Alastair appeared from nowhere. 'I'm cutting in, old man.'

Chessie did not return the masterful smile he gave her as Greg disappeared ruefully. 'That was rude,' she commented.

'Well, how else was I supposed to get near you?' he countered. 'You seem to be the belle of the ball, my sweet.' His smiling scrutiny made her feel oddly uncomfortable. 'That's an amazing dress.'

'Thank you,' Chessie said politely. 'Miles bought it for me.'

'Did he now?' His smile widened as the music changed, slowing romantically, and he put his arms round her, drawing her much closer than she wished. 'How very generous of him. But are you equally liberal in return, my sweet? Because you never used to be.'

She said coldly, 'I think that's entirely my own business.' She tried to extricate herself unobtrusively from his tight embrace, but failed. She tried another tack. 'How is your father this evening? I feel I've neglected him this week, but Miles has almost finished the book, and I've been really busy.'

'He's safely tucked up in his corner, I imagine, with Wonder Woman.' His face was suddenly moody. 'She says he's regaining more movement in his right hand every day.'

'Miles told me he's learning to write his name again.'

'Yes,' he said. 'At the most inconvenient possible moment, too.'

She stared at him in disbelief. 'Because he can prevent you selling the Court? Is that it?'

He nodded. 'Among other things.'

'Sometimes,' she said, quietly, 'I feel as if I've never really known you at all.'

'I thought you of all people would understand. After all, you know what it's like to have everything you want—only to see it snatched away from you.'

'Yes,' she said bleakly. 'I know about that all right.' She paused. 'But the Court will belong to you—one day. You just have to be patient.'

'I don't do patience very well. And I'm a bad loser. Besides, seeing you with Hunter drives me crazy.' He looked at her with narrowed eyes. 'I keep wondering how it might have been if I'd come back even a week earlier. Or if my father hadn't made me go to the States in the first place.'

What do I say to that? thought Chessie. Should I be brutally honest, and say it wouldn't have made an atom of difference? That I've known for a long time that we were wrong for each other, and tonight has confirmed it.

She said stiltedly, 'I hope we'll always be friends.' And wasn't even sure that was true any more.

'Is that all you can say?' His voice sank to a whisper. 'You could be my salvation, Chess.'

She was disturbed by the note in his voice, the way he was holding her. She was also aware that people were beginning to send them curious glances.

She said quietly and coldly, 'That's enough. Let go of me now, Alastair.' She pulled herself from his slackened grasp, and walked away.

She'd no idea where Miles had gone, but he was certainly not in the marquee, nor could she spot him in any of the groups standing on the moonlit lawn.

She went into the house, and stood looking round her irresolutely. He couldn't simply have vanished. Sir Robert, she thought, with sudden inspiration. That's where Miles might be.

But when she reached the West Wing, Nurse Taylor told her regretfully that she'd missed him. 'Mrs Cummings came for him, Miss Lloyd. He was wanted on the telephone, apparently. And I'm about to settle Sir Robert for the night now.'

'I see,' said Chessie, who saw nothing. Why on earth should anyone call Miles here? she asked herself in total bewilderment as she trailed back down the corridor. Who would even know where he was this evening?

Back in the main part of the house, the supper was being laid out in the dining room by members of the local Women's Institute, under the supervision of a harassed Mrs Cummings. When she spotted Chessie, she came darting over. 'Oh, Miss Lloyd, Mr Hunter asked me to tell you he's sorry, but he's been called away, and he'll be back later to take you home.'

'Called away?' Chessie echoed. 'By whom?'

'I couldn't say, miss.' The housekeeper shook her head. 'There was a young lady on the telephone for him, sounding agitated. And then he gave me the message for you, and went off.' She looked round. 'No, no, Mrs Hancock, dear, the desserts on the long table, please.'

Chessie, realising she was underfoot, retreated back into the hall. She could hear the distant noise of the party, and knew that she hadn't the slightest wish to rejoin it. She had no idea what kind of emergency could have made Miles rush off like that, but the fact that the summons had come from a girl fuelled all sorts of disturbing ideas.

Well, she didn't want to hang round here, waiting and wondering, she told herself flatly. She'd fetch her wrap, and go home, even if it meant burdening Mrs Cummings with another message.

One of the guest bedrooms was being used as a ladies' cloakroom. Chessie retrieved her shawl from the pile on the bed, and went out into the corridor, heading for the stairs.

'Have you gone stark, raving mad?' It was Alastair's voice, low-pitched and furious, and so close at hand that

Chessie jumped involuntarily, wondering momentarily if he were talking to her. 'Why have you got me here?'

Then she heard a familiar laugh, and froze. 'Why, darling,' Linnet purred. 'There was a time, not so long ago, when you couldn't wait to be alone with me.'

'Oh, for God's sake. That's all over. It's got to be. My father's getting better, can't you understand that? That damned consultant says he'll be perfectly capable of controlling his own affairs again, and you know what that means—divorce for you, and disinheritance for me. His lawyer's coming down next week.'

Chessie knew that she was eavesdropping, and common decency demanded that she should walk on immediately, and try to forget what she'd heard. But her feet seemed weighted down, trapping her outside Linnet's bedroom, and its half-closed door.

'But that's what we've always wanted—to be together.' There was a note in Linnet's voice that Chessie had never heard before. Fear.

'Oh, get real,' Alastair said roughly. 'We have been together—here—London—Spain. Things could have gone on exactly as they were, if you'd been discreet. He was just suspicious when he sent me off to America. But he didn't have proof, and now he does, thanks to your stupidity. You told me you always burned my letters.'

'I did—I thought I had.'

'Really?' Alastair sneered. 'Are you quite sure of that? Or did you make a unilateral decision to force the confrontation you've been pestering me about for long enough? You got your way, baby, and he's finished with the pair of us. We're out.'

'And if it was intentional, do you blame me?' Linnet hissed. 'I'm sick of pretending—of you telling me it's not the right time.'

'So you let him find out,' he said slowly. 'And it was nearly the death of him.' His voice rose. 'My God, do you realise what you did?'

'How was I supposed to know?' She sounded almost hysterical. 'He'd always been as strong as a horse. I'll never forget his face—how he keeled over…'

'Well, you're going to have plenty of time to remember it,' he said. 'But not with me. We're through, Linnet.'

'You don't mean it.' Her voice cracked.

'Yes,' he said. 'I do. I have other plans for my future. And with you out of the picture, I may even be able to talk Dad round at some point.' He paused. 'Especially if I'm married to someone he approves of,' he added significantly.

She said venomously, 'I suppose that was why you were wrapped round that little Lloyd bitch earlier. Although you didn't seem to be getting very far.'

'I'll talk her round,' he said confidently. 'When she realises Hunter is simply stringing her along, she'll be glad to turn to me again. And now we have a houseful of guests who'll be wondering where we are.'

Any minute now, Chessie thought wildly, one or the other of them was going to come out of Linnet's bedroom and catch her there. She couldn't make it to the stairs in time, so she turned, diving back into the room she'd just left.

She sank down on the edge of the bed, and stayed there, shaking from head to foot, trying to come to terms with what she'd just heard. Linnet and Alastair—secret lovers— even during that summer when she'd thought he'd belonged to her. And ever since.

She felt, shuddering, as if she'd been touched by slime. Was that all there was in the world—infidelity and betrayal? And Sir Robert too—what he must have suffered.

Oh, why wasn't Miles here, when she needed him so badly?

She froze as she realised what she was saying. Because Miles was just as bad. He didn't want her. He was using her to divert attention from his own affair. What had Alastair said—that he was just stringing her along? Had she been the last to realise this?

She got up slowly, stiffly. Outside everything was quiet, Linnet's door closed. The coast, it seemed, was clear, and she went down the stairs and out into the night like a fugitive seeking sanctuary.

The house was in total darkness when she got back, so Miles was evidently still occupied somewhere with his mystery caller. But he couldn't have gone to London, she argued as she let herself into the flat. Not if he'd said he'd return to the party for her.

I can't think any more, she told herself wearily. I'd go to bed, if I thought for one minute I'd sleep.

But sleep seemed beyond her. There was no rest for her reeling mind, so, instead, she trailed into the kitchen and switched on the kettle. She wasn't thirsty, but it was something to do. Something to fill the time.

Her coffee made, she took it into the sitting room and, curling up on the sofa, tried to watch some late-night television. But the horror film on offer failed to distract her, apart from making her wish that the sinister vampire at its centre would bite the entire cast.

Eventually, in spite of everything, she fell into a light doze.

She was awoken suddenly an hour later by the sound of the flat door opening, and voices. Sitting up, and pushing the hair back from her face, she was astonished to see Jenny walk in with Miles close behind her.

She said, 'Jen—you're back.' Then, seeing her sister's white face, and tear-filled eyes, 'What's happened?'

As she got to her feet Jenny ran forward, flinging herself at her. 'Oh, Chessie.' Her voice broke, and she began crying. 'I've been under arrest.'

'Arrest?' Chessie repeated with stupefaction. She looked at Miles who was waiting in the doorway, his face grave. 'Is it true?'

'No,' he said instantly. 'Although she has been at Hurstleigh police station, answering questions. But I swear to you, she's in the clear. No charges are going to be brought.' He hesitated. 'At least not against her.'

Chessie coaxed Jenny to sit down. She took her hands, clasping them firmly. She said, 'Darling, has this got something to do with this man you've been seeing?'

There was a pause, then Jenny nodded in reluctant assent, before hurrying into speech, 'Chess, I swear I didn't know what he was doing—not until tonight. Linda and I went out to meet him at the Millennium club. He had these tablets with him—and he wanted us to take them. Linda said she would, but I stopped her, and Zak and I had this terrible row. He was cursing me, calling me names—dreadful things. In the end, I walked out. I meant to go home with Linda, but I went back to the club instead.' Her face was pinched. 'I wanted to see him—reason with him. Only the police were there, and they were taking him away in handcuffs.' She choked. 'Because he'd sold one of those tablets to a girl, and she'd collapsed and been taken to hospital.'

'And someone told them that I was his girlfriend—that I'd been with him earlier in the evening, so they said they wanted to talk to me too. And they took me to the police station, and I didn't know what to do, so I phoned the Court and asked for Miles. And he came and stayed with me while I answered their questions, and then they let me go,' she added with a little wail.

'Oh, God.' Chessie was appalled. 'And you really had no idea what he was doing?'

Jenny pulled away. 'Of course not. What do you take me for? I'd never—never...'

'But the poor girl in hospital—what's happened to her?'

'She's in intensive care,' Miles said quietly. 'But expected to make a full recovery.'

Jenny was sobbing again, and Chessie stroked her hair, whispering soothingly.

Miles said gently, 'I think a warm drink and bed might be advisable.'

Chessie looked up at him. 'I don't like to leave her...'

He said, 'I'm here, Francesca. She'll be all right.'

She relinquished Jenny to him, and went into the kitchen, pouring milk into a pan and finding the tin of chocolate to mix with it. When she returned, Jenny had calmed a little, and was sitting with Miles' handkerchief clutched in her hand.

She gave her sister a watery smile as she accepted the beaker of hot chocolate. 'Chessie—I'm so sorry—about everything,' she added, stealing a contrite look at Miles.

'It's all right, darling,' Chessie said quietly. 'Love makes fools of us all.'

Jenny was silent for a moment. 'I may not have done very well in my exams. What am I going to do?'

'We'll worry about that when the time comes.' Chessie tried to sound upbeat, but it wasn't easy. She had taken it for granted that Jenny's future was settled, and she only had herself to worry about.

Her sister finished her chocolate, and said wanly that perhaps she would like to go to bed.

Chessie went with her to her room. 'Is there anything I can do?'

'No.' Jenny was staring around her as if she were in a foreign country. 'I—I'll be fine. Goodnight, Chess.'

She's hurting so much, Chessie thought soberly as she returned to the sitting room. And I can't make it better.

Miles was occupying the corner of the sofa, long legs stretched out in front of him. He'd discarded his jacket and tie, and unfastened the top of his dress shirt. He turned to look at her as she entered. 'Well?'

'Not good.' Chessie shook her head. There was space beside him, but she chose the small armchair at the fireside instead. In spite of her concern about Jenny, she was aware of a small fierce tingle through her nerve-endings at the sight of him, and knew it had to be resisted.

'Well, don't worry too much,' he said quietly. 'She's had

a very bad shock, and it's made her question her own judgement.' He smiled faintly. 'She'll bounce back.'

'But if she really cared about him…'

Miles shook his head. 'I think she'd already begun to have second thoughts. She may not have known exactly what he was up to, but she knew there was something wrong, and it frightened her.'

'Will she have to give evidence against him?'

'Possibly, although they seem to have enough to convict him several times over. Apparently he made a habit of targeting girls like Jenny, so that he could meet their friends and open up new markets.'

Chessie shivered. 'That's—horrible.' She was quiet for a moment, then she said, 'Tell me something—why did she send for you tonight, and not me?'

'Because I told her she could—that day I gave her a lift from school.' His tone was matter-of-fact. 'I said that if she ever really messed up, and didn't want to worry you about it, she could turn to me.' He paused. 'I got the impression then that all was not well.' He added drily, 'I'm still not her brother-in-law of choice, but at least I'm not The Ogre any more.'

'No.' She spoke with constraint.

'Another thing,' he went on. 'I think she could do with a period of stability, so it would be better if you stayed on here. Gave up your plans to be a waitress and went on working for me.'

She stared at him. 'But I'll have to move on eventually,' she said at last. 'Isn't that just delaying the inevitable?'

'Perhaps,' he agreed. 'But it will also give you more time to think about what you want for the future. The White Hart's a stopgap, Chessie. You need to consider the whole of your life.' He studied her for a moment. 'Are you even dead set on remaining in this area?'

Mutely, she shook her head. Although the other side of the world wouldn't be far enough away, if she had to live with the knowledge that he was here with Sandie Wells.

'Then I think you should allow yourself this breathing space.' He paused. 'There'll be no pressure from me. I shall be in London for the next few weeks.'

She sank her teeth into her lower lip. 'That's—very kind.' *And at the same time so bitterly, endlessly cruel.*

'That's settled, then.' There was another silence, then he said, 'I'm sorry to have left you in the lurch at the party.'

'It didn't matter.' She looked down at her hands, twisting the aquamarine ring on her finger, struggling to keep her voice level and hide the agony of emotion inside her. 'Your instinct for trouble was quite right, it seems.'

He frowned. 'But I thought it would concern the Court, not Jenny.'

'It did.' She swallowed. 'I discovered tonight that Alastair and Linnet have been having an affair for years.'

'Ah,' he said, softly. 'So that's come out at last.'

She stared at him. 'You—*knew*?'

He nodded. 'Remember the night I took you to dinner at The White Hart?'

'Yes.' She didn't just remember. Every detail was etched in her mind for ever.

'And the couple wrapped round each other in that parked car? When I met Lady Markham, I realised at once that she was the woman involved, and that she was desperate to know if I'd seen enough to identify her—and the boyfriend. When I recognised him, I became—interested.' He gave her a level look. 'So what happened? Did Alastair make a full confession in the moonlight before he proposed to you?'

She looked down at her hands. 'There was—no proposal.'

'You amaze me,' Miles said sardonically. 'I'd assumed you'd be the path back to his father's favour. So—how did you find out?'

She bit her lip. 'I—overheard something I shouldn't have done.'

'Poor Chessie,' he said. 'It's been a night of unwelcome revelations, hasn't it? Does it hurt very much?'

'Hurt?' She looked up, suddenly incredulous. 'Heavens, no. I got over Alastair a long time ago.'

Although I didn't know it, she thought, until he kissed me that night, and I wished it were you…

'It's just that I always thought they hated each other.' She shook her head. 'I feel such a fool.'

'They're the foolish ones.' He shrugged. 'They may get to spend the rest of their lives together.'

She said in a low voice, 'I don't think so.'

His lip curled. 'You mean he's decided to dump her? Could he be having conscience problems at last?'

'Yes,' she said quietly. 'Because his father found out, and that's what triggered his stroke.'

'Proving that honesty is not always the best policy.' He was silent for a moment. 'What about you, Francesca? Do you believe there's a place for secrets—or do you prefer everything laid on the line—publish and be damned?'

'That might depend on the secret.' Oh, God, she thought, he's going to tell me about Sandie Wells—that their love affair is on again—and I can't bear it. I can't…

He said, 'There's something I need to tell you, Chessie.'

She flung up a defensive hand, trying to laugh. 'Oh, no—not another unwelcome revelation, please.'

'As you wish.' His tone was level. 'Then, let's talk about something else. You're a wonderful dancer—did you know that? All inhibitions flown when the music starts.'

She flushed. 'You didn't watch me for very long.'

'No,' he said. 'I found it more disturbing than I'd bargained for. Dancing is one of the things I can't do—like playing football with the children I hope to have one day, or carrying my wife upstairs to bed. I jog along most of the time, then, just occasionally, reality bites hard.'

Her mind winced away from the images he'd created. She said falteringly, 'You have your books—a career a lot of people would envy…' *The woman you've always wanted.*

'And that should satisfy me?' he asked ironically. He

shook his head. 'It doesn't work like that, Francesca. But you really don't want to hear my plans, do you?'

'Well—it is rather late.' She got clumsily to her feet. 'And we've both had a difficult evening. You look tired.'

'Do I?' He watched her from half-closed eyes, a faint smile playing about his mouth. 'Yet sleep's the last thing on my mind.'

'All the same, perhaps you should go.' Chessie was aware she was trembling, unable to take her eyes from him. 'But before you do, I have to thank you—for what you did for Jenny, and...' She hesitated.

'And?' Miles prompted.

'And for this dress.' She looked down at herself. 'I don't think I've ever worn anything so lovely—even if it was only for half an evening. I—I'm so grateful.'

'You made it beautiful,' he said quietly.

Her voice broke. 'Please—you mustn't...'

'Why not?'

She said passionately, 'Because it isn't right—it isn't fair.'

Miles got slowly to his feet. 'You said you were grateful,' he reminded her softly as he began to walk towards her. 'Isn't it time you offered some proof?'

She said his name in a small, frightened voice, but it didn't stop him.

'All evening,' he said, 'I've dreamed of this moment.' He reached her, and his arms went round her, pulling her hard against his body. 'Chessie.' His voice was suddenly harsh, passionately urgent. 'Don't send me away. Not tonight.'

She knew that she should. But the stark, trembling yearning within her would not be denied any longer.

If this one night was all he could offer, she thought, then she would take it. Give herself this solitary memory of the few hours when he'd been hers alone to comfort her in the desert of loneliness that awaited her.

Then his mouth came down hard on hers, and all thinking ceased.

CHAPTER ELEVEN

CHESSIE'S bedroom was full of shadows, a small bedside lamp providing the sole illumination. She watched Miles close the door and come towards her, and knew that, no matter how much she wanted him, now that the moment had come she felt absurdly shy.

'You're trembling,' he said softly as he drew her towards him. He framed her face with his hands, looking searchingly into her eyes. 'Am I really so scary?'

'No. It's just that...'

'That in all the best stories, the virgin ends up with the prince, not the ogre?' He was smiling faintly, but there was a question in his eyes.

'Don't—don't ever use that word again,' she said passionately. 'Miles—I never did—I swear it...' *And you were always the prince—only I was too blind to realise.*

'I was teasing you,' he whispered. 'Isn't that allowed?'

He kissed her again, his mouth moving warmly and sensuously on hers, and she surrendered helplessly to the pleasure of it, her arms sliding up round his neck to hold him closer still.

His hand stroked her hair, and the nape of her neck, then moved downwards to release the tiny hook at the back of her dress, and, unhurriedly, to lower the zip.

Eyes closed, she stood motionless, listening to the heavy thud of her heartbeat, reassured by the gentleness of his touch.

She caught her lower lip between her teeth, tensing as he slid the straps of the dress from her shoulders, and she felt the silky fabric glide down her body, and pool round her feet.

Her hands went up automatically to cover her bared breasts, but he caught her wrists, forestalling her.

He said huskily, 'Darling—please. I—need to look at you. To remember you like this always.'

Her lashes lifted wonderingly, and for a breathless moment she studied him. In the lamplight, he seemed almost haggard, deep hollows beneath his cheekbones, and the scar a livid slash as the burn of his gaze travelled over her.

He said softly, remotely, '"But beauty's self she is…"'

That strange note in his voice sent alarm signals through her senses. Because it sounded almost like regret—as if he planned, even at this moment, to step back.

Instinct came to her aid. Chessie lifted her hands, pushing back her hair in a deliberately languorous gesture, while the smile that curved her mouth beckoned and promised.

She whispered, 'Just a few inches of lace.'

She heard the harsh catch of his breath, saw the stark yearning in his face, and then she moved, taking his hand, and leading him to the bed.

They lay facing each other. He stroked the curve of her face with his hand, then kissed her softly, fleetingly on her mouth, her eyes, her throat, and the hollow beneath her ear.

But even as her body sighed with pleasure she was conscious that Miles was still fully dressed while she was almost naked. She reached shyly to unfasten his shirt, but he captured her hand and kissed it, whispering, 'Later.'

'I don't understand…'

'Don't try,' he murmured against her mouth. 'This is all just for you.'

He kissed her, his lips parting hers in sensuous mastery, and she surrendered her inner sweetness to the invasion of his tongue, her arms sliding up round his neck, her hands tangling in his hair as she responded.

He was touching her now, his fingers tracing tiny patterns on her skin, the lightest brush of his hand making her pulses leap and throb.

The blue eyes were fixed on her face, observing every

slight intake of breath between her parted lips, the dilation of her pupils, the play of colour in her cheeks.

Each thrill of response seemed to swell and intensify, and when, at last, his hand moulded her breast, the warm, rounded flesh blossomed against his palm, her nipple hardening irresistibly under the exquisite teasing of his fingers. He bent his head, taking each rosy peak in turn between his lips, and suckling it gently.

The caressing hand moved downwards, exploring every curve and hollow, and she heard herself moan softly in mingled surprise and delight as her body moved restlessly in a growing fever of arousal and need.

His mouth covered hers, kissing her deeply and sensually in unequivocal demand as his hand pushed aside the scrap of lace and found the molten velvet heat of her.

Chessie gasped, her body arching against the intimate glide of his fingers as he stroked the core of her womanhood, exploring and inciting. Circling her tiny vibrant peak with languorous insistence as his mouth moved down to her breast.

His tongue flickering against her nipple echoed the friction of his touch against her secret heated bud. She could scarcely breathe, all her senses suspended in some limbo of anticipation. And, just as she thought she could bear no more, she was pierced by a pleasure so sudden and so fierce it was almost anguish, and she cried out as shivers of rapture convulsed her entire being.

Afterwards there were tears on her face, and he brushed them away with his lips.

'Still scared?' he whispered.

She shook her head slowly. 'Only of myself.' The thought of what he could make her do—how he could make her feel—frankly terrified her. Yet at the same time, she could feel excitement building again inside her.

He laughed softly, and switched off the lamp.

In the darkness, she heard the rustle of his clothes as he removed them. Felt the warmth of his naked skin caressing hers as he pulled her back into his arms, the points of her breasts grazing his chest, his thighs hard against her softness.

As they kissed Miles took her hand, guiding her to him, so that she could experience the stark strength of his male arousal.

'I'm not made of glass,' he murmured as his lips began a leisurely traverse of her throat.

'I'm afraid of hurting you.' For the first time in her life, she found herself cursing her lack of experience. Her total uncertainty that she could please him on this one night they would spend together.

She felt his smile against her skin. 'If you do, I promise I'll scream.' Then, with his voice thickening suddenly, 'Oh, God, yes—*yes*...'

His mouth and hands were warm and sure as they moved on her, and she felt an answering heat building inside her as she caressed him. So that when his hands slid under her hips, lifting her gently towards him for his full possession, she was not merely acceptant, but eager for this last mystery to be revealed. As he filled her, completed her in a way she had never dreamed of, she felt the breath catch in her throat.

Instantly, he paused. 'Are you all right?' His voice was shaken—urgent. 'Darling, I'm scared I'll hurt you too.'

Instinct came to her aid again. She moved, slowly and luxuriously, beneath him, hearing him gasp. 'Only if you stop,' she whispered.

At first he was gentle, murmuring endearments—reassurance—against her lips, then as she began to respond more boldly the rhythm of his mastery changed—strengthened. And she was carried with him, swept away on the flood-tide of his passion, her body as insistent—as driven, both of them aware of nothing but the rasp of their breathing, and each silken, burning thrust taking them inexorably towards their goal.

As the pleasure overtook her, overwhelmed her, she felt

herself screaming silently as each glorious spasm tore into her, wrenching her apart, tossing her like glittering fragments into a dark universe where there was only his voice, groaning her name like a prayer.

When the maelstrom receded, she lay, drained and spent, in his arms, her head pillowed on his chest. She could have remained there for ever, but she was suddenly aware that he did not share her total relaxation. That she could feel the tension radiating through him like an electric current. That he was trying to move, slowly and gingerly, his teeth gritted to hold back a groan.

She sat up. 'Miles—darling—what is it?'

'Nothing.' His voice was curt with pain. 'I'll be fine.'

'Oh, God, it's your back, isn't it?' She was suddenly frantic. 'I didn't think—didn't realise. You must be in agony.'

'A little.' There was faint laughter in his voice as his hand stroked her face. 'But the pleasure of you was well worth any torment, believe me.'

'I'll get you something—a drink—painkillers.' She reached for the lamp and switched it on.

He shifted position quickly, pulling the sheet up to cover him. 'No—I don't need anything. And turn the light off—please.'

For a moment, she was bewildered, and then she remembered the hidden scarring. The dream of happiness it had so brutally ended for him. And knew what she had to do.

She said gently, 'Miles—you've seen me naked. It's only fair if I claim the same privilege.'

His face was ashen, slicked with sweat. 'You don't understand...'

'Yes.' She bent over him, kissing his mouth. 'Yes, I do.'

Her lips moved down over his shoulder, licking the salt from his skin, and across to the hair-roughened plane of his chest, teasing the flat male nipples with the tip of her tongue.

'Nice?' She lifted her head, smiling at him.

His voice was taut. 'For a girl who lives with a writer, you have a lousy vocabulary. Chessie—are you quite sure about this?'

'Certain.' She pushed the concealing sheet down further, and stroked her fingertips across his stomach, feeling the muscles contract.

He had a wonderful body, she thought detachedly, lean, firm and smooth. Her exploring hand reached his hip and encountered the first puckering of scar tissue.

'Chessie…'

'Hush,' she whispered, touching a quietening finger to his lips. She took the edge of the sheet, and turned it back, revealing him completely. Disclosing the jagged purple lines that criss-crossed down to his thigh.

She could feel the tension in him as he waited for her reaction. For even the slightest hesitation.

She ran a caressing hand over the ugly marks, then bent her head and begin to kiss each one, her mouth soft and deliberate as it followed each twisted track.

Miles did not speak, but as her mouth and tongue became ever more adventurous she felt him relaxing.

At last he said, almost conversationally, 'Chessie, I warn you, if you go on like this, your act of compassion is going to turn into something very different.'

'So I've noticed.' Her voice quivered with laughter. 'And it's not compassion. I'm enjoying myself. But hasn't your poor back taken enough punishment tonight?'

'Probably,' he said solemnly. 'So this time I thought I'd just lie back and think of England—if that's all right with you?'

She said softly, 'Oh, I'll try to give satisfaction—sir.' And let her mouth drift gently over his hip, and down.

When she woke the next morning, she was conscious of a feeling of total well-being that was entirely new to her. For a moment, she lay still, eyes closed, letting herself luxuriate in it, dreaming a little of the day ahead, then she turned her head slowly to regard the adjoining pillow, and see if Miles was awake too.

But the bed beside her was empty. Miles had gone. His clothes were missing too, so at some point, while she'd been asleep, he'd dressed and left her quietly enough not to waken her.

Perhaps he'd decided he would be more comfortable in his own room, or maybe he thought Jenny's new acceptance of him might be tested by finding him in her sister's bed, but Chessie felt absurdly disappointed just the same.

Last night, she'd fallen asleep in Miles' arms, her sated body reduced to blissful exhaustion. Her final memory, his voice whispering to her with passionate tenderness. Surely, she'd rated a word of goodbye?

However it was Sunday, sweet Sunday, she thought, rallying her spirits. And there was nothing to stop her going over to the house and cooking him the breakfast of his lifetime.

She stretched, acknowledging the faint wincing of her muscles, then got out of bed and put on her dressing gown. Her dress was still in a crumpled heap on the floor, and she shook it out and placed it on a hanger, a little reminiscent smile playing mischievously round the corners of her mouth.

She went into the kitchen, put on the kettle, and slipped a couple of slices of bread into the toaster.

A minute later she was joined by a yawning Jenny. Her sister still looked pale, but she seemed slightly less subdued than the previous evening as she sank into a chair by the kitchen table.

'How did you sleep?'

'All right, but I had horrible dreams.' Jenny looked at her almost blankly. 'I suppose last night couldn't be one of them—please?'

Chessie patted her shoulder as she took down the coffee jar. 'I'm afraid not, honey. It was a ghastly thing to happen, but let's hope it's behind you.'

'I just feel so stupid.' For a second Jenny's lip trembled. 'I really thought he cared about me. But he just wanted me to sell his beastly drugs to my friends.'

'But you didn't.' Chessie made the coffee and handed Jenny a beaker. 'That's what you have to remember.'

'That's what Miles said.' Jenny glanced round her. 'Where is he, anyway?'

'In his own part of the house, I presume.' Chessie put the hot toast on a plate, trying to look and sound casual. 'Why do you ask?'

'Oh, no reason.' Jenny helped herself to butter, eyeing her sister. 'I didn't hear him leave last night, that's all.'

Nor did I, Chessie thought ruefully. Aloud, she said, 'Well, he's certainly not here now.' And hoped it was sufficiently ambiguous.

'He wants me to stay on for a while—go on working for him,' she continued. 'So we don't have to move out after all.'

'Well, that's one relief.' Jenny bit into her toast, and chewed in reflective silence. 'Chess,' she said at last. 'If you and Miles are getting it together, I shan't make waves. I've been a real bitch about him, I know, but that's all over, I promise.'

Chessie bit her lip. 'It's not like that. He's going away, and he needs me to act as caretaker until he gets back.'

'Oh,' Jenny said, sounding depressed. 'Is that all.'

No, Chessie thought, drinking her own coffee. But it's all I can bear to contemplate for now.

It occurred to her that one reason for Miles' absence could be that he was suffering from a massive flare-up of regret, and even guilt, having belatedly remembered he belonged to someone else.

If so, she needed to see him—put a brave face on things—assure him there would be no recriminations.

Although there might be repercussions, she thought, sinking her teeth into her bottom lip. But she couldn't allow herself to worry about that now.

An hour later, showered and dressed, she made her way into the main house. She'd half expected Miles to be in the study, but the room was deserted, and there was no sign that he'd even come downstairs yet. She went soft-footed up to his bedroom and tapped on the door. There was no reply, so she turned the handle and went in, rehearsing a teasing remark about his need for sleep.

But the wide bed was unoccupied and totally unruffled.

Chessie wheeled and ran downstairs, calling his name, only to hear her voice echo into silence.

Stop panicking, she thought. He's probably gone out for a walk, to clear his head. After all, it's a beautiful morning.

And while she was waiting, she might as well see if he'd left any work for her.

There was indeed a small pile of script waiting on the table in the study. But his portable typewriter—his talisman—had vanished with him, she realised with sudden numbness. He'd never taken it out of the house before. And that suggested with chilling emphasis that he had no plans to return for the foreseeable future.

Numbly, she picked up the script and scanned through it. He'd finished the book, but as she'd expected there was no happy ending this time either.

And then she saw the envelope lying beside it, addressed to her.

She reached for it, looking down at it, knowing with total clarity that she did not want to read what was in it. But that she had no choice. She took a deep breath, then slit the envelope open. The letter ran:

Dear Chessie,

As the book is finished, I have decided to leave for London earlier than planned. When you've finished transcribing it please send a hard copy and disk to Vinnie direct. She's expecting it.

As my plans are fluid, I've left some money for general expenses in your desk, also a letter of authorisation for the bank, if you need more.

Forgive me for last night, if you can. It should never have happened, but I can't bring myself to regret one moment. I'll remember it always.

It ended with his signature.

The sheet fell from her suddenly nerveless hand, and fluttered to the carpet. Chessie followed it, sinking to her knees and resting her head against the side of the table.

Well, she could not pretend she hadn't been warned, she thought desolately. But that was no comfort—no comfort at all.

And burying her face in her hands, she began to weep.

'Cleared out,' said Mrs Chubb. 'Gone off without a word to anyone. Well, good riddance to bad rubbish, I say.'

Chessie felt as if she'd been punched in the face. Her voice shook. 'Mrs Chubb, how dare you say that? You have no right—'

'I thought you'd be pleased.' A note of offence sounded in the good woman's voice. 'Never thought you were one of Madam's admirers.'

Chessie stared at her, open-mouthed. 'You mean— Linnet—Lady Markham has disappeared?'

'Didn't I just say so?' She gave Chessie a severe look. 'You don't seem as if you're with it, mind,' she added critically. 'White as a teacup. Are you going down with one of those nasty viruses?'

'No.' Chessie lifted her chin. Forced a smile. 'Does no one know where Lady Markham's gone?'

'Seemingly not. They were worried about telling Sir Robert, but Chubb reckons he took it in his stride. Mr Alastair hasn't had much to say either. Probably glad to see the back of her too.'

'Yes,' Chessie said slowly. 'I think you're right.' She pulled herself together. 'Mr Hunter's away for a few days, so I thought maybe we'd take the opportunity to give the study a good clean.

'I'll lend a hand as soon as I get back from posting his script.'

It was a relief to get out of the house. She'd spent the rest of Sunday completing the typing of Miles' book, and trying to evade Jenny's questions about his sudden absence.

'Did you have a fight with Miles about something?' her sister had demanded.

'Of course not.' That at least was the truth. 'He'd told me he had to go away—a combined business and research trip.' She shrugged. 'No big deal.'

'Why didn't you go with him, then?'

Chessie bit her lip. 'Because I have things to do here,' she returned. 'Besides, I could hardly leave you here on your own.'

'Yes.' Jenny gave her a level look. 'Actually, you could.' Her smile was wintry. 'Chessie—I'm not a child any more. I can cope.'

She paused. 'And you should be with Miles. I tell you, if I was in your shoes, I wouldn't let him out of my sight.'

To which, of course, there was no answer, Chessie thought now, pursuing her listless way to the village post office.

She'd seen the heavy Jiffy bag safely on its way, and was just emerging into the sunlight when she heard a voice say, 'Miss Lloyd?'

Turning, she saw Nurse Taylor smiling at her. 'Beautiful morning,' she went on with enthusiasm. 'And I'm glad to see you out and about, keeping occupied. It doesn't do to brood.'

Is she a mind-reader as well as a nurse? Chessie wondered wearily.

She was just about to enquire about Sir Robert, but the older woman forestalled her.

'Sir Robert is very concerned, of course,' she said. 'Have you heard yet when it's going to happen?'

'I'm sorry.' Chessie shook her head in bewilderment. 'I don't think I follow you.'

Nurse Taylor stared at her. 'But I meant the operation on Mr Hunter's back, of course. I understood it was to be this week.'

The familiar village street seemed to sway and dissolve. Chessie felt herself thrust down onto the post office step, and told firmly to put her head between her knees.

When she recovered, she found herself being helped to her feet by Nurse Taylor and conducted into the tearooms next door.

As Chessie was sipping with distaste the cup of sweet tea that had been ordered for her Nurse Taylor said in a matter-of-fact voice, 'I take it you didn't know.'

'No—no, of course not.' Chessie set down her cup. 'It's such a dangerous operation—I know that. Oh, how could he take such a risk?'

The older woman said levelly, 'Because it offers him the chance of regaining normal mobility, which has clearly become important to him. I'm sure you understand why.'

Yes, Chessie thought in agony. Because of Sandie Wells, that's why. Because that's the condition she imposed for resuming their relationship. And if the operation fails and leaves him helpless, she'll simply walk away. She's done it once, she can do it again.

'Why?' she whispered. 'Why—after all this time?'

'Because there's a new procedure they're going to try. My former boss at the Kensington Foundation was testing it last year, and I happened to mention it to Mr Hunter during one of his visits.' Nurse Taylor paused. 'He went up to London, and talked to Sir Philip, who agreed to operate.' She looked doubtfully at Chessie. 'I was sure he'd have discussed it with you first.'

'No,' Chessie said quietly. 'But he'll as sure as hell discuss it with me as soon as I get to London.' She took a deep breath. 'Because he shouldn't have to do this. He deserves to be loved for himself—just as he is.' *The way I love him...*

She paused. 'And I'm going to tell him so—before it's too late.'

She was sorely tempted to call at the flat on her way to the Kensington Foundation, and give Sandie Wells the tongue-lashing of her life, but she decided it was more important to get to the clinic and stop Miles taking this potentially disastrous step. Besides, if Sandie Wells had an atom of decency she'd be at the clinic too.

And I can kill two birds with one well-aimed brick, she told herself, biting her lip.

She found the Foundation's expensive receptionist frosty, and determined to protect the privacy of its patients, but she unbent slightly when Chessie told her that she was Miles Hunter's fiancée, and wasn't leaving until she saw him.

'He is scheduled for surgery with Sir Philip later today,' she was informed. 'But I'm sure you can see him for five minutes before his pre-med.'

A very junior nurse was summoned and told to conduct Chessie to Miles' private room. He was lying on top of the bed in his hospital gown, reading the paper, which he lowered to regard Chessie with frowning incredulity.

'Visitor, Mr Hunter,' the nurse announced, beaming, and withdrew, leaving them together.

Miles broke the silence, his eyes watchful. 'If you've brought me some grapes, I'm not allowed to eat anything.'

Chessie looked round the room. Miles' portable type-writer was reposing on a table in the corner, and she found the sight of it oddly reassuring. Though there was nothing else to comfort her.

'You're alone?' she demanded accusingly. 'She can't even be here for you when you're putting your life—your entire well-being on the line for her?'

'What are you talking about?' His voice was rough. 'And more to the point—what are you doing here?'

'I met Nurse Taylor in the village. She told me what you were planning.' She brushed that aside impatiently. 'And I'm talking about Sandie Wells. It's for her sake you're taking this insane risk.'

'Is it?' There was an odd note in his voice. 'I thought it was for you.'

She said desperately, 'Please don't play games because this is too serious. I know that you've been seeing her again. That she's been at your flat. And if you still want her that badly, then you must have her. I—I won't stand in your way, I swear it.

'But don't have this operation. It's too dangerous. Steffie told me what the consequences might be, and why you'd rejected it the first time. Tell this surgeon you've changed your mind. It's not too late. And if she really loves you, she'll take you as you are.'

There was a long silence, then Miles said softly, 'We need to get a few things straight. Firstly—Sandie has indeed been staying at the flat, but not with me. Some friends of mine have let me use their spare room. Secondly, she and I are not in love with each other. She and her husband have been having problems, because he wants her to be a full-time wife, and she'd like to build her career. She wanted somewhere quiet to stay while she got her head together, so I let her use the flat for old times' sake. The upshot is that she and her man have now agreed on some kind of compromise, and are giving the marriage another go. They left this morning for a second honeymoon in the Bahamas.'

He paused. 'And even if that wasn't so—if she was occupying the place for the foreseeable future, it would be inconvenient but not fatal. Because whatever we had was dead and buried a long time ago, and we both know it.

'Whereas you, my sweet prickly Francesca, are the girl I love, and the only wife I'll ever want. And I need to be your husband in the fullest sense of the word. And that's why I'm here.

'And if you love me back, now might be a good time to say so,' he added.

'I do love you—I do,' she said huskily. 'I think I've loved you always, but I wouldn't let myself accept it. And that's why I'm here to tell you that you don't need to do this awful thing—not for me...'

He patted the bed. 'Sit down and listen to me, my darling. When we first met, I was still feeling pretty sorry for myself, and bloody uptight. But then I looked at you, and I saw the saddest, most frightened eyes I'd ever seen in my life. And all I wanted to do was pick you up in my arms and keep you safe for ever. Only, I couldn't, and, just to rub salt into the wound, you tried to help me instead.' He shook his head. 'Not my best moment.'

She said, 'I remember.'

His mouth curled slightly. 'I imagine you might. But that's not the only thing. I'm so sick of it all. Sick of being in pain so much of the time, and feeling I'm only half a man.'

Her laugh cracked in the middle. 'We both know that isn't true.'

'It may not be logical,' he said. 'But it's a fact.' He took her hands in his. 'I told you, my love. I want to kick a ball with our children, and carry you up to bed. And make love to you all night long, when we get there. And for that, any risk is worth the taking.' He raised her hands to his lips. 'Besides, Sir Philip assures me the odds on my making a full recovery are much improved now.'

'You're not going to let me talk you out of this.' There were tears on her face. 'Then hear this, Miles Hunter. Whatever the outcome, I'm going to be your wife, and love you in sickness and in health—for as long as we both shall live. And nothing can change that.'

His arms went round her, and he drew her to him, kissing

her passionately. He said, softly, 'Will you be here when I wake up?'

'Yes,' she said. 'And tomorrow. And the day after for as long as it takes.'

He nodded. 'You'll find the keys for the flat in the locker drawer.'

As she found them the door opened and a nurse came in. 'Time for your pre-med, Mr Hunter.' She smiled at Chessie. 'I'm afraid you'll have to go to the visitors' room now, madam.'

'Yes.' Chessie pushed the keys into her pocket, then bent to kiss Miles, her mouth warm and sure as it lingered on his.

She whispered, 'I'll be waiting.' Then went out without looking back.

The visitors' room was comfortable, with armchairs and an array of newspapers and magazines, and she was its only occupant during an endless afternoon. Members of staff kept appearing with offers of tea, coffee and sandwiches, but she refused them all.

Each time she heard a step in the corridor outside she looked up in painful hope, and eventually the door opened and a tall grey-haired man came in, still wearing his green theatre gown.

He said pleasantly, 'Miss Lloyd—I'm Philip Jacks. I'm afraid you've had an anxious time, but it's over now, and I'm happy to say everything's gone well, and Mr Hunter will make a complete recovery.'

There were tears running suddenly down her pale face. 'You—you promise me?'

He smiled and held up a hand. 'Word of honour. He's young and tough enough to come through most things. And, of course, he has the perfect incentive,' he added drily.

'Can I see him?'

'Not for a little while. But I'll be happy to take a message. May I?'

'Yes,' Chessie said. 'Tell him I'm going out to buy a football.'

His brows rose. 'Is that all?'

'No,' she said, laughing through her tears. 'Believe me—that's only the beginning.'

The world's bestselling romance series.

HARLEQUIN® Presents

Seduction and Passion Guaranteed!

THEPRINCESSBRIDES

For duty, for money…for passion!

Discover a thrilling new trilogy from a rising star of Harlequin
Presents®, Jane Porter!

Meet the Royals…

Chantal, Nicolette and Joelle are members of the blue-blooded
Ducasse family. Step inside their sophisticated and glamorous
world and watch as these beautiful princesses find they have
to marry three international playboys—for duty, for money…
and definitely for passion!

Don't miss

THE SULTAN'S BOUGHT BRIDE (#2418)
September 2004

THE GREEK'S ROYAL MISTRESS (#2424)
October 2004

THE ITALIAN'S VIRGIN PRINCESS (#2430)
November 2004

**Pick up a Harlequin Presents® novel and you will enter a world
of spine-tingling passion and provocative, tantalizing romance!**

Available wherever Harlequin books are sold.

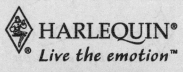

HARLEQUIN®
Live the emotion™

www.eHarlequin.com

The world's bestselling romance series.

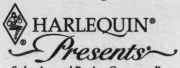

HARLEQUIN®
Presents~

Seduction and Passion Guaranteed!

Your dream ticket to the vacation of a lifetime!

Why not relax and allow Harlequin Presents® to whisk you away
to stunning international locations with our new miniseries...

*Where irresistible men and sophisticated women
surrender to seduction under the golden sun.*

**Don't miss this opportunity to experience glamorous
lifestyles and exotic settings in:**

This Month:
MISTRESS OF CONVENIENCE
by Penny Jordan
on sale August 2004, #2409

Coming Next Month:
IN THE ITALIAN'S BED
by Anne Mather
on sale September 2004, #2416

Don't Miss!
THE MISTRESS WIFE
by Lynne Graham
on sale November 2004, #2428

FOREIGN AFFAIRS... A world full of passion!

**Pick up a Harlequin Presents® novel and you will enter a world
of spine-tingling passion and provocative, tantalizing romance!**

Available wherever Harlequin books are sold.

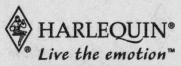

HARLEQUIN®
Live the emotion™

www.eHarlequin.com   HPFAUPD

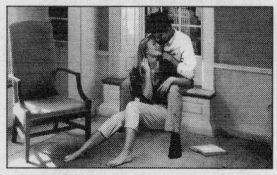
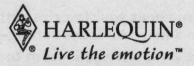

Receive a FREE hardcover book from

HARLEQUIN ROMANCE®

in September!

**Harlequin Romance celebrates the launch of
the line's new cover design by offering you
this exclusive offer valid only in September,
only in Harlequin Romance.**

To receive your
FREE HARDCOVER BOOK
written by bestselling author
Emilie Richards, send us four
proofs of purchase from any
September 2004 Harlequin
Romance books. Further details
and proofs of purchase can be
found in all September 2004
Harlequin Romance books.

*Must be postmarked
no later than October 31.*

**Don't forget to be one of the first
to pick up a copy of the new-look
Harlequin Romance novels in September!**

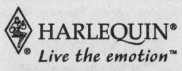

Visit us at www.eHarlequin.com

HRPOP0904

The world's bestselling romance series.

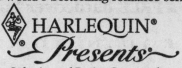

HARLEQUIN®
Presents

Seduction and Passion Guaranteed!

Legally wed,
Great together in bed,
But he's never said...
"I love you"

They're...

Wedlocked!

**The series
where marriages
are made in
haste...and love
comes later....**

Don't miss
HIS CONVENIENT MARRIAGE by Sara Craven #2417
on sale September 2004

Coming soon
MISTRESS TO HER HUSBAND by Penny Jordan #2421
on sale October 2004

**Pick up a Harlequin Presents® novel and you will
enter a world of spine-tingling passion and
provocative, tantalizing romance!**

Available wherever Harlequin books are sold.

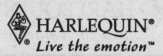

HARLEQUIN®
Live the emotion™

www.eHarlequin.com   HPWEDSO

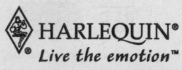